The Carrollian Tales
of Inspector Spectre

The Carrollian Tales of Inspector Spectre

R.I.P. (Restless in Pieces)
by Byron W. Sewell

ILLUSTRATED BY THE AUTHOR
WITH AN AFTERWORD BY EDWARD WAKELING

AND

The Oxfordic Oracle
by Byron W. Sewell
and August A. Imholtz, Jr

ILLUSTRATED BY HARRY FURNISS

evertype
2011

Published by Evertype, Cnoc Sceichín, Leac an Anfa, Cathair na Mart, Co. Mhaigh Eo, Éire. *www.evertype.com*.

A catalogue record for this book is available from the British Library.

ISBN-10 1-904808-81-6
ISBN-13 978-1-904808-81-7

Typeset in De Vinne Text, Mona Lisa, ENGRAVERS' ROMAN, and *Liberty* by Michael Everson.

Edited by Michael Everson.

Illustrations to *R.I.P.* (*Restless in Pieces*): Byron W. Sewell, 2011.
Illustrations to *The Oxfordic Oracle*: Harry Furniss, 1889, 1893.

Cover: Michael Everson.

Printed by LightningSource.

Foreword

I first started writing *R.I.P.* (*Restless in Pieces*) in early October 2009. I was well into it when I received a call at work on the 22nd of November 2009 from my wife, Victoria, informing me that she had just read an article by Margaret Nighbour on *news.scotsman.com*, that a thumb and finger bone from the corpse of Galileo Galilei's corpse, which had been stolen in 1737 as his body was being moved to a new tomb, had been purchased at auction by a private collector. My immediate reaction was that everyone who read my story would believe that I was inspired by that. I wasn't.

As if that wasn't bad enough, I had no sooner finished writing the initial draft of this story when on the 11th of December 2009 I read in the news that the body of former Cyprus President Tassos Papadopoulos (at one time reputedly a leader of the Greek Cypriot guerrilla group EOKA) had been stolen from his grave. The article included this quote:

> "What happened is macabre and utterly condemnable. I am honestly still trying to comprehend what kind of warped minds could even think of doing such a thing, let alone actually carry it out. This is a perverse act that will sicken society in Cyprus," said the head of Cyprus' ruling AKEL party, Andros Kyprianou.

Again, I feel compelled to say that I was not inspired by this news account. However, I was intrigued by the rhetorical question asked by Mr Kyprianou: "...*what kind of warped minds could even think of doing such a thing...*" Well, I suppose the obvious answer to that question is now "minds like Byron Sewell's." I want to assure everyone, including the Cypriot police, that I had nothing to do with the Papadopoulos crime.

The publisher and I are grateful to Edward Wakeling for permitting us to publish, here for the first time, his fascinating article about what most likely actually happened to Dodgson's missing diaries, one of the great literary mysteries. Edward is a true-life sleuth, whose abilities far outshine those of the fictional Inspector Spectre.

Following *Restless in Pieces* is a second tale, "The Oxfordic Oracle", which is the brainchild of August A. Imholtz, Jr's wildly comic imagination, which never ceases to entertain and amaze me.

Special thanks to Ivor Crumble, an expert on all things British, for his highly-valued advice.

Byron Sewell
Hurricane, December 2011

CONTENTS

R. I. P.
(Restless in Pieces)

An *Alice* Sesquicentennial Tale

BY
BYRON W. SEWELL

ILLUSTRATED BY
THE AUTHOR

C H A P T E R   I

Planning

*T*oby and Brian took a train from Victoria Station and arrived in Guildford late in the afternoon on an overcast day in early October. The air was crisp with a hint of fall and the low grey clouds hid most of the sunshine. They walked along High Street to The Mount, where they slowly climbed the hill along the narrow paved roadway until they reached the tall outer stone wall, sections of which were topped with ivy, that enclosed the old Victorian Guildford Cemetery. They stopped at the cemetery entry and briefly studied the modern wrought iron gate that had been hung on relatively new red brick posts that had been integrated into the old Victorian stone wall, to see how difficult it would be to scale it when the cemetery was closed and locked for the evening. The large blue sign just inside the gate informed them that the cemetery would be closed at 18:00, which gave them about an hour to look around.

They passed though the gateway and stopped awhile to scan across the old graveyard, which was somewhat devoid of larger trees except around the perimeter wall. It was crowded with row upon row of old tombstones, some of which had tumbled from neglect over the years. Across the cemetery they could see Booker's Tower, an early-Victorian four-storey structure, looming outside and over the perimeter wall, its gabled top vaguely shrouded by the mist of the low clouds drifting across the cemetery in the gloom. They walked along the paved roadway towards what had originally been the cemetery chapel, but now St Michael's Russian Orthodox Church. Almost directly in front of the main doors to the church they noticed a little green and white sign planted in the lawn along the pathway that pointed them at what they were looking for, Lewis Carroll's grave.

They walked over to the grave and studied the distinctive white cross that served as Mr Dodgson's tombstone, erected many years ago by his brothers and sisters. The grave was well-tended, with a ground cover of small flowers, all framed by a low concrete curbing that defined the limits of the plot. The grave was now hard against an ancient cypress that dominated this section of the cemetery, towering well over eighty-feet into the mist of the low clouds. In fact, it was now so close to the base of the tree that the ground and grave curbing had been lifted up by the tree's roots. "That's a problem," Toby said, pointing at the base of the tree. "There's bound to be large roots what 'ave grown over and through the casket. We'll need to bring a saw and axe."

As they stood at the foot of the grave, a group of three very excited and animated Japanese tourists appeared. Toby and Brian moved away to let them have room to start taking dozens of photographs of themselves standing next to, in front of and behind the tombstone, their cameras whirring and flashing like paparazzi taking photographs of a famous celebrity. Finally satisfied that they had enough photographs of the grave they turned their cameras on the surroundings, snapping photographs of everything of possible interest: St Michael's Church; the graves beside Lewis Carroll's own grave; the big cypress standing sentinel-like next to his grave; Booker's tower in the distance; and, even the little green sign that identified Lewis Carroll's grave-site. At one point one of them took a copy of a paperback *manga* translation of *Alice in Wonderland* out of her backpack and set it on the base at the foot of the cross as a votive offering to Mr Dodgson's spirit, hoping that he might intercede with some higher power on her behalf for a grandson.

Brian and Toby left them to their photographic indulgence and walked around the cemetery, memorizing the layout and pathways so that they would have no problems returning to the grave-site on some foggy night when they wouldn't be able to see much further than a few feet in front of them. Brian was particularly interested in knowing where they might be able to scale the back wall in case the police unexpectedly showed up and they had to make a run for it. When they left the cemetery twenty-minutes later they noticed that the trio of enthusiastic Japanese Carrollians were still taking photographs with reckless abandon; laughing and jabbering away at each other like mad things.

Having descended The Mount they crossed back over Portsmouth Road to the base of High Street and turned south down Bury Fields along the west bank of the river to The Walrus and Carpenter, a recently refurbished Fuller's pub. A few years ago this had been The White House, named for the main entryway that featured a portico that resembled the White House in Washington, D.C., except that it was almost on a dollhouse scale in comparison and had only four columns. The pub had gone on economic hard times due to bad on-line reviews of its food and because of the rise in anti-American sentiment, which had blossomed due to the Middle-Eastern

misadventures of the two Bush administrations and especially when President Obama had promised to end the wars in Iraq and Afghanistan, but only made things worse, committing even more American troops, and dragging along more British troops with them. In order to try to salvage the pub, Fuller's had hired a design firm to give the pub a distinctly English atmosphere. They had renamed it The Walrus and Carpenter in honor of Lewis Carroll, Guildford's most famous dead person, buried up on The Mount overlooking the city.

Brian and Toby tried to enter the ground floor through the portico, but found it so crowded that they couldn't make their way through the press and opted to walk around to the side and take the spiral metal staircase to the second floor. The large pub sign on that side of the building had once featured a painting of the American White House, but now displayed a Tennielesque scene of the Walrus, Carpenter, and oysters. Even the second floor was crowded, but Brian and Toby were eventually able to work their way up to the bar and ordered pints of Fuller's Pride, the London brewer's famous premium ale. Eventually, a tiny oval table opened up and they were able to take a seat.

"Cheers!" Brian said to Toby, holding up his mug, when they had sat down.

"Cheers!" Toby said and downed half of his pint in a single swallow.

"So, Toby, now that you've seen the grave, what do you think?"

"The big tree will definitely make it harder to get to the casket. It's a bloody shame the bloke wasn't buried in one of the graves what was out the open!"

"Yes, but it's just what it is."

"Isn't there someone else who's famous what we could dig up instead?"

"None that I know of. The advantage to Carroll is that the grave-site is unguarded at night by anything except the front gate. We should have a full night undisturbed. I don't want to have to bash some guard's 'ead to give us access."

Toby nodded. "We'll give it a try. Like I said, if we bring a saw and axe I suspect that I can cut through the roots, but it will be tough going." He drank the rest of his ale. "I'll have another round," he said. "How about you?"

"No, I'm fine." Hungry, Brian picked up a sodden menu, also decorated with Tenniel's familiar Walrus and Carpenter *Looking-glass* characters to see if there was anything he could afford. The menu featured fresh oysters on the half-shell, flown in daily by air to London's Billingsgate Market and then trucked to Guildford the same day: bluepoints, Apalachicolas and Malpeques; salty Belons; sweet Gigas; and even mild Japanese *kumamotos*. It was enough to make a hungry walrus swoon, but all at outrageous prices and far beyond the means of all but the wealthiest walrus. There was also the normal pub fare of Shepherd's Pie and Bangers & Mash, but even those were priced for the tourist trade and also well beyond Brian's meager means, so he finally just turned the menu over and tried not to think about food.

After another two pints Toby finally allowed that his thirst was somewhat quenched and they headed back to the station to catch the next available train to London. Unable to get seafood off of his mind, they stopped at a small fish-and-chips shop on the way and Brian settled for that more plebian fare. Toby wasn't hungry.

For the next several weeks Brian went on-line and checked the weather forecast for Guildford on the BBC Weather website for Surrey until he finally learned that dense fog was forecast for Guildford on October 31. This time the pair returned to Guildford in Brian's old Telecom van, via the A3 and A3100, arriving late in the afternoon. Brian parked the van in a public lot and they returned to The Walrus and Carpenter to down a few pints to build their courage and wait for the fog to roll in. Brian was a light drinker and had only two pints of Newcastle Brown. Toby, a former semi-pro boxer, who was all muscle and weighed slightly more than 16-stone, quaffed six pints of Fuller's Pride and was still able to walk a more or less straight line when they left The Walrus and Carpenter to commence their nefarious activities.

CHAPTER II

Meeting

*T*he front-page banner on *The Natural Inquisitor* in the magazine rack at the Wal-Mart checkout lane in Hurricane, West Virginia was even more outrageous than usual, which was saying something:

LEWIS CARROLL'S GRAVE ROBBED!
SKULL AND 3 FINGERS TAKEN

Not believing that it could possibly be true, Tucker Nipp burst out laughing so loudly that the red-headed woman in front of him, who was struggling to write a cheque, messed up her own signature. She turned on Tuck like a cornered possum, hissing, "Look what you jest made me do!" She shoved her checkbook an inch in front of Tuck's face; so close that he couldn't focus on it. "I don't got no free checkin and this'll cost me plenty!"

Tuck was taken aback by the venom in her tone of voice. "Sorry!" he said. "How much?"

"How much what?"

"How much will that ruined check cost you?"

"How'n blazes 'm I suppost to know?"

Tuck offered some friendly advice, "You can get free checking, you know."

"Sure, iffen you got a big balance in yer account. I ain't."

Tuck dug into one of the leg pockets on his deer hunting camo-jeans and produced a quarter, which he handed towards her. "My apologies, ma'am; I couldn't help myself when I saw that funny headline."

She snatched the coin as quickly as a starving Bombay street urchin. "Keep the change," he thought, but didn't dare say it.

"What headline?" she snarled.

He put a finger on *The Natural Inquisitor*. "This one"

She shoved Tuck's cart backwards a few feet so that she could see the newspaper better. "What's so danged funny about somebody robbin a grave? You got a strange sense a humor!"

"No, I don't! Hey, that's as funny as the last issue, which featured a photograph of some guy in a Big Foot costume eating a Big Mac!"

"That could happen," she argued. "Maybe it killt a camper and stole her lunch."

"Yeah, I suppose anything's possible." It struck Tuck odd that she had assumed that the camper was a woman and wondered if something like this might have actually happened to her in the past. He had read numerous accounts of people across the Ohio River swearing that they had encountered a local monster in the woods. "Have you ever encountered Mothman?" he asked.

She looked hard at him, as if she was trying to decide whether to tell him or not. "Well, I did see something strange with big red eyes one time up Turkey Crick, but I ain't sayin thet it was Mothman. It was too dark to see for certain. I don't rightly know what it was, but it were huge and stunk somethin terrible; like it was dead! I shore hope I never smell thet thing agin! Could'a been Mothman, for all I know. I flung a big rock at hit an screamed as loud as I could. When I did thet it took off a-runnin through the woods. You could hear hit a-crashin through the booshes all the way down the hill and acrost the crick on tother side."

"It might have been a bear," Tuck suggested.

"Bar's don't stink thet bad!"

"It would if it had been eating a old deer carcass. Bears will eat almost anything."

"Bars don't got red eyes. You ever see a bar with red eyes?"

"Maybe it had an eye infection," Tuck suggested.

"Look! It weren't no bar!"

Tuck nodded and decided to change the subject. "By any chance do you happen know who Lewis Carroll was?"

Her eyebrows knit together as she tried hard to remember something that seemed only vaguely familiar. "Cain't say as I do," she finally allowed. "He from round here?"

"No. He's been dead since 1898. He's buried in England— at least part of him still is, if that headline is true, which I doubt. He wrote *Alice*."

"Alice who? You ain't makin no sense! You tryin to rile me up?"

"No, no! I sure don't want to do that! By *'Alice'* I meant *Alice in Wonderland.* I'm sure you must have read that story at home when you were a child."

"No, I ain't read hit. When I was a kid we was real poor; we didn't have no books at home, cept *The Bible* and I could'n understand much of thet, what with all them thees and thous and thines! As I recall it also had lots of don't do this and don't do thet in it, too."

"*The Bible* was the only book in your house?"

"Well, we had an old Putnam County phone book, but thet don't count, I reckon."

"No, I wouldn't count that. Well, *Alice* is a famous children's story. Lewis Carroll wrote it almost 150 years ago."

"What the heck you talkin bout? Everbody knows he did'n write thet story."

Tuck glanced over at the cashier, who was as happy as a ground hog munching a bologna sandwich, since they had the check-out line jammed up and she could take a short breather. Tuck turned back to his adversary, noticing for the first time that her bare arms were strangely masculine and muscled-up, just like the photographs that he'd seen on-line of Madonna's arms. Also for the first time he noticed that she had a tattoo of a strand of barbed-wire wrapped around her left bicep. He guessed that she'd probably got that while she was spending some time in the women's pen up at Alderson and couldn't help but wonder if she might be dangerous, since Alderson was where West Virginia sent most of the state's murderesses. Still, he couldn't just let it go by that someone actually believed that Disney had written the original *Alice*. "Lewis Carroll definitely wrote that story," he insisted.

"No he did'n. Disney wrote it. I got the 50th anniversary CD to prove hit!"

"Disney just made a movie out of it. He didn't write it. That CD is just the 50th anniversary for the movie."

"You sure bout thet?"

"Positive. I'm surprised that you don't know that."

Her eyes narrowed and the barbed wire stretched a little as her large biceps flexed. "You talkin down to me, mister?"

"No, ma'am. I just assumed that someone your age would know that."

"Oh, really? And jest how old you think I am?" Tuck suddenly had a mental image of her whipping a hunting knife out of her bra and slicing up his face. He figured that she was at least fifty, but decided to lie through his teeth and aim low, since some people who lived a hard life up the hollers sometimes looked much older than they really were. "I'd guess you're maybe twenty-seven; twenty-nine tops."

Without warning she smashed her bony fist into Tuck's chest. "Go on!"

Tuck yelped like a stepped-on Chihuahua at the sudden, unexpected pain in his flabby right pec. "Look, I'm not good at guessing women's ages," he said as he rubbed his bruised chest; "maybe you're only twenty-five; I don't know."

She hit him again, this time even harder, and then surprised him with a big come-on grin. The cashier thought this was unbearably funny and couldn't help but snicker. A Wal-Mart manager, who had noticed that the line in their lane wasn't moving, stomped over and interrupted them. "Excuse me, Sir! You two need to move on. You're holding up the checkout line!"

Tuck looked back over his shoulder into the very unhappy faces of three middle-aged women. He noticed that the one nearest to him was wearing a black tee-shirt with a very evil-looking, gothic Cheshire Cat emblazoned across her ample bosom. He was particularly struck by the fact that the cat's very pointed teeth were dripping blood. The lady at the end of the line yelled up at them, "Hurry up, will you? My ding-danged ice cream's gonna melt back here!"

Tuck turned back to the manager. "I'm not the problem. I'm waiting on this nice lady in front of me to write a check!"

The manager turned to her and said, in as pleasant a voice as he could manage under the trying circumstances, "Ma'am, I'd appreciate it if you would go ahead and pay for your beer." Tucker noticed that she had eight 24-count cartons of Budweiser stacked up in her cart, along with a giant bag of Cheetos sitting on top of them. As far as he could tell there wasn't any actual food in the cart.

She gave the manager a look hard enough to crack a rock and Tuck expected her to reach over and bust his lip for him, but to his surprise she turned and obediently started writing a new check. "Thank you *so* much, ma'am," the manager said to her, in a rather sarcastic tone, "for shopping at Wal-Mart!"

"You ain't freakin welcome, you creep!" she possum-hissed at him. "Next time I'm shoppin at Krogers! You jest lost yersef a valuable customer!"

The manager ignored her meaningless consumer threat and turned back to the irate ladies-in-waiting. "Checkout lanes 15 and 16 have just been opened for your shopping convenience. You might want to move over to one of those while these two happy Wal-Mart shoppers sort out their issues. Thank you all for shopping at Wal-Mart!"

The woman in the menacing Cheshire Cat tee-shirt said, "Next time I'm goin Krogerin ma-sef!"

Tuck reached over and pulled all six available copies of *The Natural Inquisitor* out of the rack: one for his own personal collection of strange Carrollian ephemera (which just happened to be his primary collecting focus), and the five others to send to some other more-or-less-normal collectors who lived in Maryland, England, Canada, Germany, and Japan. He figured his friend August might spot a copy while he was shopping for Altoids and ginger ale in a Seven-Eleven, but he was pretty sure that the others wouldn't.

The fascinating tattooed red-head finished writing her check and smacked it down hard on the counter, making a sound not unlike a small pistol being discharged. An elderly lady in the next lane over flinched and grabbed at her chest. The cashier ran the check through the machine that verified whether the check would bounce (it didn't) and handed her a receipt. "You have a nice day, darlin," she said in a surprisingly sweet voice. She gave her a big smile and then told her, "I'm not supposed to tell you, but Krogers has better beer prices anyway. You should check it out."

"I'll do thet! Thank you."

Tuck managed to get checked out without further incident, though he took a bit of grief from the cashier, who asked, "Twenty-five?" and then snickered. "Right! And I'm eighteen!"

Tuck started to say something smart back at her, but decided he was already in enough trouble as it was and wisely kept his mouth shut.

On his way to his pickup Tuck inadvertently walked by the feisty redhead as she was unloading her beer into the back of a beat-up old Plymouth Caravan. He tried to just sneak quietly on by without being noticed, but she spotted him out of the corner of her eye and spoke, "Hey bud, you want a Bud?" She effortlessly ripped the top off of a cube, pulled out a can and held it out to him.

Tuck thought it would be best to accept the beer gracefully and avoid a fist-fight in the parking lot, certain that he would lose. He hated fighting anyone, men *or* women, with big biceps and small, boney hands that seemed to go right through you when they hit you. "Don't mind if I do," he said and then struggled unsuccessfully to pop the top. She jerked it away from him and effortlessly popped it. "Thank you!" he said and took a sip. "My name's Tucker; Tucker Nipp. That's Nipp with two P's. Most of my friends just call me Tuck."

She smiled. "Mine's Jake."

Tuck's first thought, based on her strange muscular Madonna-like arms, was that he or she might be a transvestite. "Really?" he asked. She nodded. He decided to give her the benefit of the doubt. "You're the first woman I've ever met named Jake."

"Now ain't thet a co-inky-dink? You're the first man I ever met what's named Nip and Tuck! You ain't a plastic surgeon by any chance are you?"

"Not Nip and Tuck! Tucker Nipp."

"You serious?"

"Yes. My name's a bit unusual; I'll admit that."

"Yeah, a bit!" She laughed. "Kinda cute though."

"How'd you come by Jake?"

"Mom named me Jada, but my Daddy didn't like hit; he said hit sounded too oriental. He's still mad about Pearl Harbor, I guess. So he started calling me Jake, just to pull Mom's chain. He liked to rile er up fer some reason; I never rightly figgered out why. Mebbe hit had somethin to do with their love life. Anyways, 'Jake' stuck. You can call me Jake."

"Personally, I like Jada better. Would you mind if I called you Jada?"

"No, I don't mind. You can iffen you want to."

"Do you live close by, Jada?"

"Sorta. I live up Turkey Crick. You ever hear o Turkey Crick?"

"As a matter of fact I have," he lied. "Well, I've got to get going. It's been nice meeting you, Jada. I'm sorry about your check. Thanks for the beer."

"What was the name of thet guy what you said wrote *Alice in Wonderland*?"

"Lewis Carroll. You ought to read the original version sometime, Jada. I think you'd like it. It's better than the movie. Disney messed with the story quite a bit. They're sure to have a copy of it in the Hurricane Public Library; even that little branch over by the Middle School should have it."

"Like what did Disney mess with?"

"Well, for instance, in the original story the Cheshire Cat wasn't purple with pink stripes."

"It weren't? What was hit then?"

"The book doesn't say, but the illustrations of it make it look like an ordinary gray and black tabby."

"No kiddin?" She thought about this for a moment. "Actually, I like Disney's version better. Thet cat was pretty funny when his stripes come undone."

Tuck nodded. "Most Americans would agree with you, but the English hate Disney's version."

"Why's thet?"

"Well, they regard the original version of the story as sort of sacred and don't really like it when anyone messes with it."

"What? Like hits the *The Bible* or somethin?"

"Yeah, sort of, I suppose; the Bible of Children's Books."

"Maybe I *will* git me a copy of the original an give hit a read," Jada said. "Hit got any thees and thous in hit?"

"None that I recall."

"Well, thet's a good start."

Tuck nodded. "Perhaps if I see you around again sometime you can tell me what you thought of it."

Her eyelids suddenly drooped and she smiled, revealing the tip of her tongue, all of which had the effect of totally unnerving Tuck. "You ever drop in at the Southern Pride Lounge over on Route 60?" she purred, as if she didn't want anyone to overhear her. "I go in there some weekends fer a brew or two. You do too and you jest might see me there."

Tuck knew the Pride. He drove by it everyday on his way to and from work. It was a hideous two-storey cinderblock building painted grey and blue.

There were usually a few pickups and a 4-wheeler or two parked out front on the gravel. At least one of the pickups would usually have a Confederate flag design in the rear window. All of them would have at least one decal that had something to do with deer hunting or fishing, and most of them had rude or crude bumper stickers. "No, I've never been inside the Southern Pride."

"Why's thet? You ain't no Yankee, are you?"

"No. Actually, one of my great-grandfathers was a Rebel. The fool joined Wall's Legion down in Texas to fight and like to got himself killed at the fall of Vicksburg over in Mississippi. He was wounded three times, but somehow managed to survive. He almost starved to death during the siege and had to eat horses and rats. He must have been a tough old bird!"

"Heck! You'd fit right in at the Pride! You oughta give it a try! Tell them boys bout yer great-gran-pappy and they'll likely buy you a beer and a order of the Pride's famous flamin-hot chicken wings."

"No, I don't think I would want them to do that. I'm more of a Wal-Mart kind of guy," he assured her. "I mostly drink caffeine-free diet Dr Pepper and eat peanut butter and banana sandwiches."

She ignored this bit of very disappointing information. "I'm usually at the Pride on Friday nights after nine. My D-Q shift ends at eight on Fridays."

Tuck smiled. "OK. Maybe I'll drop by the Pride sometime for a few minutes."

"I'll look fer you."

Tuck smiled. "Good-bye, Jada."

"You come on by the Pride now, Nip Tuck!" she persisted.

He smiled again. "Not this weekend, Jada; I'm too busy."

"Doin what?"

"Oh, this and that. I've been working for years writing a guide to collecting *Alice in Wonderland* figurines. It keeps me busy. There must be a thousand different ones, and every single one of them is some kind of ugly. It's quite fascinating, really."

A strange expression came across her face, as if she had just run over a skunk. "You serious?"

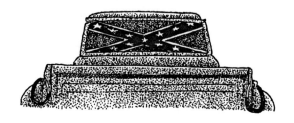

He decided that he'd better lie again. "No, not really! I was just joshing you. I don't give a hoot about *Alice* figurines." The truth was that he had over 500 of them in his collection, and as far as he knew, he had more than anyone except Joel Birenbaum who, at last count, had 859 and was recorded in the *Guinness Book of World Records* for his amazing achievement.

"You had me worried there fer a minute, Nipper!" she said and then laughed. Then her voice got low again, "Well, iffen you git yerself un-busied then come on by the Pride. We'll have a good ol time—you an me. I might even wear one of them *Alice in Wonderland* costumes I seen on eBay, you want me to. Dress up like her fer you sometime. You'd probably like thet, would be my guess."

Tuck momentarily imagined her in one of those skimpy costumes he'd often seen on eBay while he was surfing for obscure Lewis Carroll stuff, and decided that he probably would. "You'd do that?" he asked.

"Maybe. We could play mad tea-party or somethin."

Tuck took a long drink from his Bud. "What size do you wear?" he asked. "I'll buy it."

She laughed and then said, "Dream on, Alice! I was jest foolin with you, Tuck. I ain't puttin on one of them fool things—not fer you or my husband neether!"

That caught him by surprise. "You're married?" Tuck swallowed hard.

"Yeah, that's him a-sittin in the driver's seat up front there. It's right hard to see him in the dark, since the dome light's burnt out, but he's a-starin right at you; probly wonderin why you're a-drinkin his beer and talkin to me."

Tuck peered into the dark interior of the old van and saw a black shape that vaguely reminded him of The Hulk. "Thanks for the beer!" he said to the Hulk-shape, then turned to Jada and said, "I better go now."

"Yeah, I reckon," she agreed. "Iffen you want to keep all of yer teeth."

Tuck hightailed it to his pickup and left a little rubber on the Wal-Mart parking lot asphalt as he peeled out. In his hurry he managed to nail a shopping cart and sent it careening across the parking lanes and into a post. He didn't stop.

$\mathbb{P}$ i q u i n g

$\mathcal{W}$hen Tuck got home from Wal-Mart he immediately turned on his laptop and checked Yahoo! News to see if there was any mention of Mr Dodgson's grave having been disturbed. Sure enough, there it was, under the "Odd News" category:

"Off with his head!"— Grave-robbers nick Lewis Carroll's skull on All Hallow's Eve

By Xie Kitchin Etté

Reuters UK Friday Oct 31, 2014 5:00 am ET

GUILDFORD— In an ironic literary twist, Detective Inspector Ian Spectre, on-loan from the London Metropolitan Police Service, announced today that the grave of Mr C. L. Dodgson, the real name of Lewis Carroll, the famous author of *Alice's Adventures in Wonderland*, *Through the Looking-glass* and *The Hunting of the Snark*, was disturbed overnight, and his skull is missing. DI Spectre indicated that a preliminary inventory of the casket contents indicated that along with the skull, three finger bones from the right hand that Mr Dodgson would have used to write his stories with were also missing.

All twenty of Guildford's Police Constables have been interviewing nearby residents today to see if anyone noticed anything suspicious going on last evening. PC Throttlemartin told this reporter that there was a thick fog all evening after 22:00, which he felt certain would have obscured and muffled the sounds of the digging. One resident, who wishes to remain anonymous, who lives close to the cemetery boundary near Booker's Tower, claimed that he had heard what sounded like someone chopping and sawing wood about 03:00, but had thought nothing of it and had gone back to sleep.

The grave-robbers were somewhat thwarted in their efforts to steal the entire body, since the casket was entangled by the thick roots of a nearby large cypress. The grave site was left in a mess, with the famous white cross grave marker tipped over and the grave still open. Sections of large roots that had been thrown onto the lawn gave testament to the difficulty of getting to the casket and evidence of the grave-robbers' determination. They had finally had to settle for uncovering only the top part of the casket, the remainder being hopelessly entangled.

The Lewis Carroll Society (London) has offered a reward of £42, along with an inscribed copy of one of Lewis Carroll's more obscure and oft-maligned works (a bizarre fairytale entitled *Sylvie and Bruno Concluded)*, along with a rare and valuable set of Victorian magic lantern slides of *Alice in Wonderland*, for information leading to the arrest and conviction of the perpetrator(s).

DI Spectre suggested that the purloined bones will most likely be smuggled into America, where there are unscrupulous and extremely wealthy Lewis Carroll collectors, some of whom would probably be willing to pay handsomely for the literary relics. However, when pressed for the names of

these collectors, he steadfastly refused. Police inquiries are continuing.

Tuck then checked *The Times* on-line and found a similar, though considerably longer, article about the crime, along with a brief biography of the Lewis Carroll that was riddled with famous and persistent errors and myths (e.g., he hated little boys, he once sent a logic book to Queen Victoria, he had an affair with the real Alice's mother, he stammered in front of adults but not little girls, he owned a pet dormouse named Euclid, etc.). The bit about the dormouse was new to Tuck. *The Times* had even interviewed Dr Selwyn Goodacre, a past-Chairman of the Lewis Carroll Society.

"I have long maintained that the Rev. Mr Dodgson's remains should have been disinterred and removed to Poet's Corner in Westminster Abbey, near the plaque that the Lewis Carroll Society erected in his honour. The Society's Memorial Plaque Committee pleaded that this be done, but the Abbey authorities insisted that there simply wasn't enough room left in the Abbey to even provide a decent burial for a cricket. Now look at what's happened! If they had only done what we asked then this heinous crime could not have been so easily committed. We are hopeful that the Lewis Carroll Society of North America, many of whose members are reputedly fabulously wealthy, will offer a substantial reward for information leading to the return of Mr Dodgson's remains. Our own English Society has put up a modest reward, but we simply don't have the necessary means to pay a high ransom demand should one be forthcoming. Most of what little money we had accumulated over the past fifteen-years has been spent on publishing Mr Dodgson's *Diaries*."

There were numerous similar articles in other on-line newspapers—even in various foreign languages (German, French and Canadian)—to name just a few and, of course, the blogs were in full cry, replete with various conspiracy theories, though most agreed that some sort of ransom demand was the most likely outcome. One prominent Italian blogger speculated that the Naples Mafia might somehow be involved, and another far-left blogger in Massachusetts blamed it all on former President George W. Bush, whom he pointed out, was a member of the secretive Skull and Bones Society at Yale, along with his father, former President George H. W. Bush.

Tuck sat and thought about the possibility of owning the Reverend Mr Dodgson's skull. "It would be illegal, of course," he told himself, "and even if I did manage to acquire it I could never let anyone know that I had it; but wouldn't it be wonderful? Other collectors might own inscribed books, manuscript letters, original photographs—Charles Dodgson's boyhood toys—furniture from his rooms at Christ Church— even his cribbage board—but what could compare with owning his *actual* skull? The skull that probably still contained the desiccated remains of the *very* brain of the genius that had created the *Alices?*" His mind spun off like a tee-totem in a kind of mad, ghoulish reverie. He pictured the skull encased in an elaborate golden shrine, like the reliquary of some obscure medieval saint—perched atop a bookcase filled with rare first editions inscribed to his child-friends.

Then he began to wonder about the skull's condition. "Would there be bits of skin remaining? Would it be enough for some mad Korean geneticist to attempt to clone him like they had recently done with a baby mastodon? Would there be tufts of grey hair? Would it be better to clean the skull or leave it as it was found? Where would I keep it? Obviously, it would have to be out of view." He thought about possibilities: "In a gun safe here in the house? No, someone might break in and steal the safe, thinking it contained money or drugs. Perhaps I could keep it in my safe deposit box down at the bank down in South Charleston. No, some bank clerk might get a glimpse of it and think it was the head of someone that I had murdered! Much too risky! Perhaps in the attic? No one ever went up there. No—I would have to think of something cleverer than that!" Then he started thinking about repercussions should the police find out that he had it in his possession. "Would there be hard time in a Federal penitentiary or just a light sentence with white collar climate-criminals like the disgraced data-rigging Dr Hansen with whom I would play golf every afternoon?"

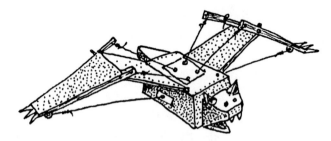

After thinking about such things for awhile he finally snapped out of his delirium, telling himself aloud, "It's moot, Tucker! The thieves are hardly going to contact you and make you an offer! And you certainly don't have any idea of how to contact them! You might just as well wish that you owned the original Bob the Bat! Put it completely out of your mind!" It was good advice; he knew it. Still it was fun to think about the possibility of owning the ultimate, unique Carrollian collectible and he couldn't help himself. There might be something like twenty-five first editions of *Alice*, but there was only *one* skull!

CHAPTER IV

Counting

*B*rian Mome was a frail man in his early thirties, whose most distinguishing attribute was a set of remarkably horrible teeth. However, genetics *had* dealt him a reasonably good brain and a fair education allowed him to do most of the thinking for the pair's petty criminal endeavors. His partner in crime, Toby Rath, provided any necessary muscle—heavy lifting, digging, or even roughing someone up a bit.

At first Toby and Brian weren't at all sure what they had found in the casket besides Mr Dodgson's bones, but Brian had a hunch that they might be worth a bob or two. One was an old biscuit tin carefully wrapped in oilskin that contained a rather mildewed and warped copy of *Alice's Adventures in Wonderland*. He noted that it had the date 1865 on the title page. The other was a diary, also wrapped in oilskins, whose first entry was dated April 15, 1858. The diary's leather covers were well worn and had a few unfortunate ink splatters, one of which had a shape that vaguely resembled a pig with wings. Its pages were foxed and it had a quite noticeable mildew odour, but the contents were still quite legible, the oilskins having protected it reasonably well from damp and worm.

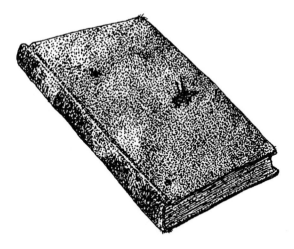

Brian told Toby, "We shouldn't be too hasty in trying to flog these. The last thing we want to do is to take them into some used bookstore to see what they might offer us for them without having any idea of their true value. I'll go on-line and see if I can find anything out about them." He began a search and a few minutes later exclaimed, "Crikey! The bleedin book might fetch £50,000 at auction! Even though it's a bit shabby!"

Toby leapt to his feet at this unexpected news and shouted, "Brilliant!"

After enthusiastic high-fives they settled down to consider the diary.

"Well, it's most likely Charles Dodgson's, since it's buried with him. Give me a few minutes and I'll see what I can find on-line." He typed in "Lewis Carroll" and immediately hit the Lewis Carroll Homepage, where he soon figured out that they had discovered what might well be one of four missing volumes of Mr Dodgson's diaries. He looked up at Toby, who was now peering at the laptop screen over Brian's shoulder. "It seems that our Mr Dodgson kept a diary most of his life. Four volumes went missing many years ago. We have apparently found one of them! It could be worth a million!"

"Really?" Toby asked, his eyebrows arched and his eyes wide in disbelief.

"Maybe. Who knows?"

"What was it doing in his grave?"

"No way to know. My guess is that someone discreetly placed it there, along with his famous book, just before they closed the lid and put him under."

"You'd have to be barmy to bury a book worth 50,000 quid and a diary worth a fortune!"

"When they buried him the book was probably only worth a few shillings, so it was no big deal."

"Who would've done it?"

Brian shrugged. "I don't know. He had some old maid sisters that he took care of for most of their lives. Maybe it was one of them. Again, there's no way to know such things. Everyone alive at the time of his funeral is in his or her own grave by now. The secret has probably gone with them. But it sounds like something a sister might have done."

"But why would she want to do that?"

"People do sentimental stuff like that at funerals; you know, put a favourite toy in the casket with one of their kids what has died young, to keep him company in his grave. Or a husband leaves a valuable diamond ring on his dead wife's finger."

"I wonder if anyone will leave something in me own casket when I croak?"

"Tell you what, Toby, if I'm still alive and I can make it to your funeral I'll slip in a few bottles of Ridgeway Bitter—just in case you wake up in the dark and get thirsty." He grinned at Toby.

"Ha! Ha! Very funny!"

Brian laughed.

"Who would want to pay a million pounds for an old diary?" Toby asked.

"I imagine that it would be almost priceless to someone who collected Lewis Carroll. Our problem is that, apparently, none of his diaries has ever appeared on the antique book market, so its real value is unknown. We'd have to auction it to find out."

"You mean on eBay?"

"No, I mean like at Sotheby's or Christie's! This isn't just any old book! We need some big fancy auction house where people spend millions for old paintings."

"So, what would we do? Just walk in and tell some bloke that we want to auction it?"

Brian shook his head. "It's not likely to be that easy. We're going to need a good story about how we came to have such a valuable object in our possession. The fact that we've had several convictions for larceny will make them wonder. And, anyway, they'll want to have the book and diary appraised and inspected by experts to determine if they're genuine."

"So when can we do it?" Toby had already started to think about what he might buy with the money.

"I think that we need to wait six months or so before we try it."

"Why so long?"

"The police might put two and two together and guess we plundered it out of Dodgson's grave if we rush to do it. And then it might be another two or three months until the sale date. No doubt it'll be a long wait, but well worth the waiting! What we need to do is to build some cover."

"Like what?"

Brian thought about it for a few minutes.

"I've got it! We should go into the used book business."

"What? I don't know nothing bout old books! I've only ever read two books all the way through in me whole life!"

"You don't need to know anything about books. I'll take care of it. We'll rent a little stall in some antique mall—maybe on a side street off Portobello Road. We'll buy a few hundred cheap old books and mark them with high prices, so that no one will actually buy them. Titles wo'n't matter. I'll only open the stall on Saturdays, so it wo'n't be too painful to sit with it for a few months. I know! We'll call our shop Jubjub Books and have a sign painted. We'll probably need a licence. There's no tax or VAT on secondhand books, so we wo'n't need a licence to collect tax. Once in awhile I'll buy a book from someone who comes in to flog it and be sure that other people in the stalls see me do it, so it looks like we're actually in business. That will make us look legit. Then one day you'll put on a disguise and come in and offer to sell me the old *Alice* and the diary. I'll act like I don't know you and I don't know what they are. I'll talk loudly and be sure that the other stall keepers hear me. I'll go on and on about how they're dirty and smell like damp. Then I'll offer you twenty quid for the lot and you'll take it and leave. I'll put the books in an old bag and pretend that it was just an ordinary sale."

"Then what?"

"I'll take them into some fancy rare book dealer—Maggots or Querulous or somebody like that—and ask them to appraise the books. I'll get a receipt. It might cost us something like £30 for the appraisal. They'll tell us what we already know, but I'll act surprised. Dance a little jig in their shop. Whoop and holler. I'll take their appraisal and the books to Sotheby's or Christie's and put them up for auction. If the police come to interview me, which they probably will do, I'll tell them that a man came into Jubjub Books and wanted to sell them, and that I gave him twenty quid for the lot. They'll want witnesses. I'll give them the names of the other stall keepers around my stall. They'll confirm my story and we'll be home free. They'll want to know the name of the man who sold them to me, but I'll tell them I have no idea. Never saw him before in me life."

"What if someone sees that we're friends and tells the police?"

"That's why you have to come in disguise. And it has to be a good one!"

"Only one problem that I can see." Toby said.

"What's that?"

"We don't have the money to get started—to buy the books for stock, the licence, the rents, the signboard, the appraisal—all that stuff."

"That's true enough."

"How much do you think we'd need?"

"Four or five hundred pounds should do it."

"That much? Where are we going to get all that then?"

"We'll ransom Dodgson's bones for the full amount."

Toby nodded. "So who do we send the ransom note to?"

"The Lewis Carroll Society. I've got their mailing address right here on-line on their homepage. Even if they wo'n't pay it themselves they'll probably know how to get in touch with some of Dodgson's relatives, who'll probably pay it. Once we get the money we'll dump the bones off somewhere and tell the police where to fetch them. Bob's your uncle!"

Toby smiled. "It just might work!"

"Course it will!"

"What say we celebrate with a pint!"

CHAPTER V

Cleaning

*T*wo weeks later Brian and Toby met again in Toby's
bedsit. Brian, who was wearing latex gloves, came in
carrying a plastic bucket in which there was a zip-lock
polythene plastic bag, a padded mailer (on which he had
already attached an address label for the Lewis Carroll
Society and a fictitious return address, along with more than
enough stamps for the postage), a small plastic bottle with
some motor oil in it, some paper towels, and an extra pair of
latex surgical gloves. There was barely enough empty floor
space to spread things out and for them to sit down.

"Now this is important, Toby!" Brian explained. "We have
to be very careful not to leave any fingerprints on *anything*,
and I mean anything! So, put on these gloves and get the bone
box out from under the bed. I haven't touched any of this stuff
with my bare hands, so they're clean."

Toby put on the gloves and drug out the cardboard bone box.

"Get out the finger what's still got some skin attached and
put it in the bucket," Brian instructed.

Toby did as he was told, but to his dismay, the finger fell apart into three pieces when he dropped it. "Sorry!" he said. "No worries. The Dodgson family will no doubt call in the police when they receive the ransom note and the police will know finger bones when they see them. I'm going to pour this oil all over the bones to contaminate any fingerprints that we might have left when we took them out of the casket. Then I'll wipe them off with a paper towel and then drop the bones into this plastic bag." Brian did this. "Here's the note," he said, pulling it out of his shirt pocket. It was already bagged and Toby could read through the clear polythene.

THIS IS DODGSON'S FINGER. YOU CAN COMPARE ITS DNA WITH WHAT'S IN HIS CASKET. LEAVE £500 IN OLD UNMARKED £10 NOTES IN AN ENVELOPE AT THE BAR IN THE WHITE HART ON MARYLEBONE AND BAKER ON 15 DEC. WRITE: "FOR COLLECTION—DINAH" ON IT. NO POLICE OR ELSE NO SKULL.

Toby handed it back to Brian, who inserted it along with the bones into the mailer, which he then sealed.

"Now what?" Toby asked.

"I'll take the tube and drop this into a pillar box somewhere far from here. Can you take all of this other stuff and toss it into a rubbish bin somewhere?"

"Sure."

"Remember to wear the gloves! If you leave fingerprints on anything the police will sooner or later be knocking on our doors. Don't save anything! Everything must go into the dustbin. Do you understand? Every single thing! Once you've disposed of that take off the gloves and throw them away somewhere else—like a public loo. Understand?"

"Yes, I understand, but there's one other thing."

"What's that?"

"We need to find someplace else to keep the bones."

"Why? Nobody will come in here and look under your bed."

"It's not that."

"What is it then?"

Toby hesitated. "Well, strange things have been happening ever since I brought them bones in here. I'm getting a bit spooked."

Brian laughed. "Are you worried about Mr Dodgson's ghost?"

Toby wasn't smiling. "I don't believe in ghosts. Still, strange things have been happening."

"Like what?"

"Well, me light bulb burned out."

"That's what eventually happens to all light bulbs, Toby!"

"I know, but this one was only a day old."

"I'm sure that it was just a manufacturing defect. It happens."

"Ever happen to you?"

"Well, no," Brian had to admit. "That it?"

"No, there's more. One of me socks disappeared!"

Brian couldn't help laughing again. "That happens to everyone, Toby, including me. That's why I only buy black socks; that way the ones I have left always match! No one knows where socks go. They just disappear. I assume they get lost at the laundry. It's one of the great unsolved mysteries of the universe. Scientists have been working on it for centuries. Even Einstein couldn't figure it out!"

"I put the socks on the floor beside me bed. When I woke up, one was gone! I didn't take it to the laundry. It should have still been there when I got up."

"Well, that does sound a bit strange," Brian admitted. "Perhaps you walk in your sleep and don't know it and you took it off outside."

"I don't walk in me sleep!"

"How do you know?"

"I just know."

Brian couldn't see any point in arguing about this, so he dropped it. "Anything else?"

"Yeah. It gets worse. Last night I heard something scratching around under me bed. It sounded like it was coming from inside the box what have the bones in it. I got up and turned on the light and pulled it out. When I did, the scratching noise stopped! I looked inside the box and it was just the bones."

"So, if I understand you correctly, you're thinking that one of Dodgson's fingers was scratching the box trying to get out?"

Toby shrugged. "I know that it sounds barmy. Still, I 'eard what I 'eard!"

"You've probably just got a mouse," Brian suggested, "what was scratching to try to get into the box. It could probably smell the bones and thought it smelled like food."

"I don't have mice. I've set traps, but caught nothing. There's no droppings. If you've got mice you see their droppings!"

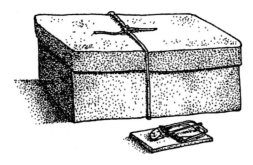

"Well, then I assume you were dreaming and the sounds you heard were just in your mind, since you know that the bones are under your bed. Dreams can seem very real at times. I'm sure that there is a rational explanation."

"I don't dream."

"Of course you do. Everyone dreams!"

"I don't. I lay me head on the pillow and then I wake up, usually many hours later. I have no memory of anything; not even time passing. I've never had a dream that I can remember."

"That's very odd! I dream every night and sometimes they're so vivid that I wake up more tired than when I went to bed."

"Like I said, we need to find somewhere else to hide the bones. You take them back with you and put them under your bed if you want to. I ca'n't sleep with 'em here and I'm not sleeping out in a park!" He pushed the bone box towards Brian.

"Give it another night, Toby. Stiff upper lip! If something else strange happens then I'll take the box back with me and pop it under my bed. Not to worry."

C H A P T E R   V I

E s c a l a t i n g

Two days later the mailer containing Mr Dodgson's finger bones and the ransom note was delivered to Mark Richards' home, since he was the current Chairman of the Lewis Carroll Society and all Society mail was automatically forwarded to him. Without thinking too much about it, he opened the mailer and discovered the ghoulish contents and ransom note. He immediately rang DI Spectre.

"Detective Inspector Ian Spectre speaking. How may I help you?"

"My name is Mark Richards. I'm the current Chairman of the Lewis Carroll Society. I don't believe that we've ever met. I was given your name and phone number by the Guildford Police in case the Society heard anything from the scum who robbed the Mr Dodgson's grave. In this morning's post I received a package containing what is purported to be the bones form one of Mr Dodgson's fingers. My wife, who is a surgeon, has assured me that they are genuine finger bones."

"Was there a ransom letter?"

"Yes."

"Typed or written out in longhand?"

"Typed. Looks like it was printed out on a computer. It's in a plastic bag. I can read it through the clear polythene.

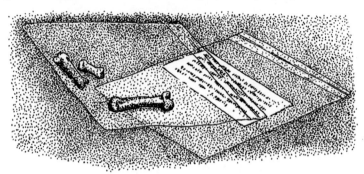

"How much do they want?"

"Five hundred pounds."

"That little? That's odd. I was expecting more. Please don't touch anything further, Mr Richards. We will have it analysed for fingerprints."

"I've already opened the mailer and touched the plastic bag with the note, so my fingerprints will be on things. Sorry. I wasn't expecting anything quite like that. But the bones and note are in polythene bags, so I haven't touched those."

"That's fine. Just don't handle it any further and don't let anyone else handle it either. I'll send over a forensics technician to retrieve it. She will also need to take your fingerprints so that we can distinguish any you might have left. She'll bring a kit."

"Quite! I wo'n't let anyone else touch it, not that I think anyone would even want to! I must say that it's rather eerie to see Mr Dodgson's bones, even if they're just from one of his fingers!"

"Yes, I'm sure. I'll try to drop by later this afternoon for a brief chat as long as something urgent doesn't delay me. In any event, I'll be back in touch as soon as I can."

An hour later the technician arrived to pick up the mailer and to take Richards' fingerprints. She was quite efficient and was gone in less than ten-minutes. An hour later DI Spectre knocked on the front door and Richards invited him in. "Do come in, Inspector. It's a pleasure to meet you in person."

They shook hands. "I wo'n't take but a few minutes of your time, Mr Richards."

"We can talk in my office. Right this way Inspector, if you please." He offered the DI a seat in front of his desk.

"This is a nasty business," the DI said; "quite uncivilized. Some people will apparently do anything for money these days, though it is unusual in modern times to be dealing with grave-robbers."

"I suppose that it probably has something to do with drugs," Richards suggested. "It seems that almost every modern crime has drugs involved in it in one way or another."

"Yes, it is a contributing factor in many cases," the DI agreed, "but there are other possibilities, such as gambling debts. There's no way of knowing at this stage."

"When will you have results from the tests?"

"It will take a few weeks to do the DNA testing. However, we will know quite soon if they find any fingerprints. Frankly, I doubt that whoever did this would be so foolish as to leave them."

"Do you expect that the bones are genuinely Mr Dodgson's"

"Yes, I imagine that they are, though we will need to confirm it, of course."

"What should we do about the money they have demanded?"

"That is entirely up to the Dodgson Estate. I would appreciate your contacting the Executors for me at your earliest and ask them how they wish to proceed."

"Actually, as it happens, the Dodgson Estate is managed by two women, who are rather distantly related to their famous antecedent. As you probably know, the Reverend C. L.

Dodgson was a bachelor, so there are no direct descendents. His extended family takes care of his literary estate."

"Do you expect that the Estate will be willing to put up the ransom money?"

"Perhaps. Can the police put up the money?"

"Unfortunately, we are not in a position to supply the money from our very tight budget. I'm sorry. Perhaps the Lewis Carroll Society might be willing to do this in Mr Dodgson's memory."

"I don't know. We are a relatively small not-for-profit literary society. In the event that the Dodgson Estate ca'n't or wo'n't put up the money I will make inquiries to see. This is all quite upsetting for many members of the Society, as you can imagine. I suspect that something can be worked out. We shall wait until I've had a chance to discuss this with the Estate."

"That's fine. Please let me know what you learn as soon as you can."

"Of course. I'll ring you immediately I know anything."

"You should advise anyone you talk to about this matter to keep it confidential. Unfortunately, things do often leak out to the press, which I feel certain they would like to avoid."

"We certainly don't want to stir up the tabloids, especially since we are fast approaching a major anniversary and really don't want a lot of negative press."

"Which anniversary might that be?"

"The sesquicentennial of the publication of *Alice's Adventures in Wonderland*."

The DI did some quick mental math. "That would be 2015, if I'm not mistaken."

"Precisely. The celebrations will require lots of money. That's another reason why the Society can not really afford to commit a large sum of money at this time to something in which it might simply be lost!"

"I understand. Well then, I look forward to hearing from you in the near future. I'll take my leave now."

"I'll see you to the door, Inspector."

CHAPTER VII

Menacing

$\mathcal{T}$oby returned to his bedsit once the Red Lion had closed. As usual he had drunk too much, yet he did manage to get his shoes off before falling onto the bed. He was sound asleep almost immediately.

At about 03:00 he was awakened by loud groaning noises that seemed to be coming from under his bed. He sat up and shook his head in an attempt to clear his mind. The groaning continued so he got out of bed and switched on the lamp on the table by the bed. The groaning ceased. Nonetheless, he got down on his knees and slowly lifted up  the bedspread so that he could peer into the darkness at the bone box. After staring at it for a few minutes he decided that it must have all been his imagination. He switched off the lamp and crawled back onto the bed. "That's it!" he said aloud. "Them bones be going to Brian's! No excuses. He either takes 'em or it's the dustbin!" He was soon back to sleep.

He didn't wake up again until daylight was streaming in through the small window high on one wall. He forced himself to sit up on the edge of the bed and when he glanced over at the pillow at the head of the bed he leapt to his feet and raised his fists in a fighting stance. There on the top of the pillow sat Mr Dodgson's skull. He would have recognized it anywhere, since it had near-perfect white teeth, something quite rare in Britain on either a live or a dead person.

He fumbled around until he found his cell phone and rang Brian. "It's Toby. I need you to get over here. Right now!"

Brian could tell that he was stressed out by something. "What's wrong?"

"Never mind! Just get over here as quick as you can!"

It took Brian about ten minutes to get there. He knocked on the door, not sure what to expect. When it opened he saw that Toby's face was pale and drained. "Are you ill?" he asked as he came in and closed the door behind him. Toby shook his head. "What is it then?"

"The skull."

"What?"

"There! On the pillow!"

"There's nothing on the pillow, Toby."

Toby reached over, grabbed Brian by his shirtfront and effortlessly pinned him to the wall. "Dodgson's skull is sittin on top of me pillow!" he said, with genuine menace.

"Let go of me!" Brian demanded. "Let go! What are you talking about? The skull's in the box under the bed!"

"It's not! It's in plain view. Where I say it is!"

"There's no skull there, Toby! You're just seein things."

"Are you sure?"

"Yes." Brian walked over to the pillow, picked it up and shook it. "See? Nothing!"

"You shook it off! It's laying over there in the corner!" Toby was pointing at it. "There!"

"There's nothing there, Toby. You're hallucinating."

"I am?"

"Were you doin any drugs last night, Toby?"

"No!"

"OK, well then suppose you tell me what happened last night."

"Last night I was at the Red Lion till closing. I had more than a few beers and came home pissed. I was sleepy, so I landed on me bed and was soon asleep. In the wee hours of the mornin I hear this loud groanin noise under me bed, what wakes me up. It doesn't quit, so I finally gets out of bed, turns on the light and takes a look under me bed. The groanin instantly quits. I don't see nothing. After awhile I think I must have been dreaming, even though I ca'n't remember having ever dreamed in me whole life. I go back to bed. I guess I must have finally gone back to sleep, because when I wake up it's morning. I look over and see the skull sittin there on top of me pillow and it looks like it's looking at me! It's *his* skull! I know it!"

"Whose?" Brian asked. "Dodgson's?"

"Yes, whose do you think? The one what we nicked in the graveyard!"

"No way!"

"Yes, way!" Toby snarled.

"Let's have a look to see if the skull's still in the box."

"*You* want to know what's in the box then you check. I ain't touchin it!"

Brian reluctantly got down on his stomach and retrieved the box, which he very cautiously opened. When it was fully open they both saw the skull, right where it had always been. Toby jumped up and stared at the corner again, but the skull was no longer there.

"How'd the skull get back in there?" Toby demanded.

"It never left, Toby. You're hallucinating. Perhaps you're drinking too much."

Suddenly, one of the finger bones rolled over in the bottom of the box. It might as well have been a snake. Toby and Brian both jumped back from the box. "Crikey!" Brian screamed. They both stood with their backs against the wall, their pulses racing. "You know, we could both use a drink," Brian finally said.

"True, but the pubs aren't open yet."

"Oh! Yeah, right! I forgot what time it is." He was silent for a moment, then he said, "Fancy a cuppa? I'll treat. Frankly, I'd like to get the hell out of here!"

"For the first time this morning I agree with you!" Toby replied. "Let me grab my shoes and we're out of here."

A few minutes later they were sitting in a café, sipping their tea, and their pulses were still racing. "So, Brian, you're the brains of this outfit. What are we going to do with them bones? Like I said, they're sure not staying under my bed!"

"I don't know, Toby. I'm not keeping them under my bed either! The only place I can think of is in the garage I rent for my van, but that's not very secure. Someone might break in and steal them."

"That would be just fine with me," Toby said. "They'd be welcome to 'em!"

"But we need the money! We ca'n't just pitch them somewhere."

"Then it seems to me that the only other alternative would be to keep them in your van."

"I wouldn't feel safe driving around with those bones in the back of the van. What if they attacked me while I was driving?"

"My guess is you'd be dead; head-on crash or something."

"Yeah. So, I guess we stash them in my garage."

"I don't have a better idea."

CHAPTER VIII

Arranging

Two weeks later Mark Richards rang DI Spectre. A woman answered. "Metropolitan Police Service. May I help you?"

"I'd like to speak with Detective Inspector Ian Spectre, if I may. This is Mark Richards. I urgently need to speak with him if at all possible."

"One moment, please, Mr Richards. I'll check to see if the DI is available. Please hold the line."

"Thank you."

A few minutes later DI Spectre came to the phone. "Mr Richards? Spectre here."

"Good day, sir. I've had a talk with the Dodgson Estate."

"Yes?"

"They're willing to pay the ransom. However, they don't want the police to interfere, since if something goes wrong then their chance at getting the bones back for a relatively small price would be lost."

"It's a bit of a gamble. They might lose their money and not recover the bones."

"They know that. But they are simply unwilling to pay even a penny more. I will collect the money and deliver it to the White Hart on the 15th of December if you would like me to do it."

"Before you do I would appreciate your recording the serial numbers on the bank notes for us."

"I'll do that, but I repeat, Inspector, the Estate doesn't want police interference. They want the bones back."

"We wo'n't interfere until you safely have the bones back. If the money eventually shows up in circulation we may be able to find out who spent it. We might even be able to recover some of it, though I don't want to hold out too much hope for that happening."

"Yes, I see. Very well, as long as I have your word on it."

"You have my word. By the way, I strongly advise you to leave the pub immediately after you deliver the ransom. Under no circumstances should you confront any of them. Though I think it unlikely, they might be armed and dangerous. We know they have no morals to constrain them. Normal people do not rob graves, so there is no way to know what they are capable of!"

"Believe me, Detective Inspector, I have no intention of confronting them. I shall leave the pub immediately after the delivery. But if they do attack me I am quite able to defend myself. I would rather enjoy busting a few heads."

"I certainly hope that it doesn't come to that. Please let me know the outcome of the affair as soon as you can."

"I certainly will, Detective Inspector, though I don't expect to know anything until they tell us where to collect the bones."

Richards rang off.

DI Spectre called one of his men into his office, where he explained the situation. "Arrange to have a hidden surveillance

CCTV installed at the White Hart as soon as possible, well before the 15th of December. Direct it at the bar. We'll activate it on the 13th and let it run until the 17th. Don't tell the pub management why we want it; just say that it is police business and that we appreciate their cooperation. We might get lucky and catch one of the perpetrators on video. Do not interfere in the actual pickup. I assured Mr Richards and the Dodgson Estate that we would not do that."

"Very good, Sir," he said and left the DI's office to make the necessary arrangements.

On 15 December Mark Richards dropped off the envelope containing the ransom at the White Hart.

CHAPTER IX

Following

*B*rian walked into the White Hart in the crush of the lunchtime crowd. One of the lads behind the counter finally asked him, "What'll it be, mate?"

Brian put a £20 note on the bar. "A envelope for collection was left here early this morning. This twenty is yours if you will drop the envelope in the trash and take it outside and dump it with the rest of the trash into the garbage bin."

"You serious?"

"Yes, quite serious. There are some embarrassing photos in it that I really don't want my wife to see. Her name's Dinah. Her name is supposed to be written on the outside of the envelope."

"Yeah, I see it. OK. I'll dump the trash in about an hour." He took the twenty and slid it inconspicuously into his pocket.

"Brilliant," Brian said and left. "Thanks."

Forty-five minutes later, Toby and Brian were still watching the White Hart's delivery door when a man came out with a bulging black polythene bag and pitched it into the garbage bin. "That's him," Brian told Toby. "I'll go get the van."

Once Brian had left, Toby walked over to the bin and retrieved the top bag and carried it over to Marylebone Road where Brian was waiting at the curb. Toby pitched the bag into the back of the van and they drove back to Brian's garage. They closed the door and then opened the bag. They dug around until they found the envelope.

"Yes!" Brian said, greatly excited.

"Success!" Toby echoed.

Their euphoria was short-lived. The envelope had been ripped open and inside it there was a wadded up dishcloth. It would be an understatement to say that they were disappointed.

"Do you know the guy's name?" Toby asked.

"No, and what's more the bastard took my twenty!"

"So, now what?"

"Let me think for a minute." Brian thought and thought, then finally said, "The people what put up the ransom are going to think that we took the money and now they'll want the bones back. I ca'n't blame them. Here's what we do. Tomorrow you watch for the guy who took our money leave from work. Follow him until you get his home address. Once we have that I'll make an anonymous phone call to Crimestoppers and tell them that he's the one what robbed the grave. With any sort of luck they'll catch him with some of the ransom money. They might even find a marked note on him, I wouldn't be surprised."

"What about the bones?"

"I'm not sure. We'll wait and see what happens first."

The next day Brian and Toby returned to the White Hart and looked for the guy who had stiffed him. He finally came in for work about 10:00. Brian pointed him out and then left. Toby didn't much like the idea of waiting around all day for him to go home, so he went around back and waited for him by the trash bin. An hour later the bartender stepped out with a bag of garbage and Toby punched him hard in the face. "May I see your driving licence, sir?" he said as the man crumpled to the loading dock. He deftly reached into his pocket, found his wallet and took out his licence, but left everything else, even his cash. Before he left he kicked him in the ribs, fracturing three.

An hour later Toby knocked on Brian's door.

"Toby! What are you doing back already? You're supposed to be tailing that jerk so we can find out where he lives!"

"I got tired of waiting so I asked him for his driving licence." He handed the driving licence to Brian.

"You asked him for this?"

"Well, technically I punched in his face and asked him for it while he was falling to the paving. I'm not sure that he heard me, but I did ask him."

"You didn't kill him did you?"

"I don't think so, but I'm pretty sure that I cracked a few ribs for him as I was leaving."

"Why didn't you just tail him?"

"I got tired of waiting."

"After only an hour or two?"

"Yeah; I hate waiting."

"Can he identify you?"

"Not unless he takes my driving licence away from me, and I'm not too worried about him doing that. He's got a glass jaw."

"Did anyone see you assault him?"

"I don't think so."

Brian looked at him in unbelief for a few moments. "Well, what's done is done. I'll go find a public phone somewhere and call a tip into the police." He took out a tenner and handed it to Toby. "Why don't you pop down for lunch on me?"

"Brilliant," Toby said as he turned and left.

Brian copied down the name and address on a scrap of paper then cut up the licence into tiny bits, which he would drop in a bin on his way to find a public phone.

He rang 0800 555 111.

"Crimestoppers. May I help you?"

"Yeah, I want to leave an anonymous tip."

"One moment, please. I'll just connect you to the recorder."

While he waited he took out a handkerchief and carefully wiped the receiver to remove any prints, holding it the rest of the time with the cloth. Finally a voice came on. "At the sound of the tone you may leave a message." This was immediately followed by a tone. Brain slowly and distinctly said, "The bloke what dug up Lewis Carroll's grave in Guildford is George Bander and lives at Eastend Terraces, Building Six, Flat 1106." He then dropped the receiver and quickly left.

DI Spectre received the information from Crimestoppers ten minutes later. He called his assistant into his office. "We have a tip from Crimestoppers identifying the Mr Dodgson's grave-robber as one George Bander. He gave an address. Sign out a vehicle and let's pay him a visit."

It took them an hour to make their way through London traffic to the address, a concrete and glass tower of low rent flats provided as public housing. They parked and went up to the eleventh floor and knocked on the door of 1109.

"Who is it?" asked a woman's voice from behind the door.

"Police. Please open the door. We would like to talk with you for a minute."

"Do you have a warrant?"

"No, ma'am, it's not that sort of situation. We just want to talk with Mr George Bander. Does he live here?"

They waited for her to unbolt four locks and open the door a crack. She looked frightened.

"You needn't be afraid, ma'am. I am Detective Inspector Ian Spectre of the Metropolitan Police." He then held up his identification for her to see. "This is PC Eggleton. Can we come in rather than shout at you through the door? You might not want your neighbours to hear everything that's said."

The door opened wide. "George isn't well, but come in."

"Are you Mrs Bander?"

"Not technically. We aren't married, but I live here."

"Is Mr Bander ill?"

"He was punched out at work. We just returned from surgery."

"What are his injuries?"

"A mild concussion, three fractured ribs and a few missing teeth."

"Have you reported this assault to the police?"

"No, George don't want to press charges. I told him he should, but he refuses."

"Why is that?"

"I don't know. He just refuses."

"Where does he work?"

"He tends bar at the White Hart on Marylebone Road."

"Is he well enough to talk to?"

She shrugged her shoulders. "I guess. He seems to be able to order me about without much difficulty."

"Can you ask him to come in here?"

"I don't think he'll be able to do that. His ribs are killing him. It takes him ten-minutes of effort just to sit up. Follow me and I'll show you into the bedroom." They went in. "Georgie, this here's the police. They want a word with you."

"I told you not to call them!" he snarled.

Spectre interrupted them. "She didn't call us. We are here as a result of an anonymous tip that says you were involved in a recent crime in Guildford."

"Where's Guildford?"

"In Surrey."

"I've never been there."

"Mrs Bander has told us that you were assaulted. Do you have any idea why someone might have done that?"

"No. I was just emptying the trash at the pub where I work and this bloke blind sides me with a hard right to my jaw. I lost two teeth. He must have kicked me while I was down. I have three cracked ribs. I can barely breathe, much less move and I have a splitting headache."

"Were you robbed?"

"He took my driving licence."

"That's all?"

"Yes."

"No money taken?"

"No."

"Have you recently come by a large sum of money?"

"I won £500 betting the horses."

"Did you report this windfall as income to HM Revenue and Customs?"

"Not yet, but I plan to."

"Do you have these monies here on the premises?"

"Yeah. I didn't make it to the bank as yet because of me injuries."

"I would like to examine the money, please."

"Why?"

"I need to check some serial numbers."

"Why?"

"We'll discuss that in a minute after we've had a chance to look at the serial numbers."

"It's in that envelope over there on the top of the bureau."

With the help of PC Eggleton, Spectre compared the serial numbers with the list provided by Mark Richards, and quickly found that the numbers on all of the notes except one £20 note matched. He walked back over to the bed. "Mr Bander I am placing you under arrest."

"On what charge?"

"Disturbing a grave, extortion and obstruction of justice."

"You must be barmy!" George said and tried to sit up, but screamed from the pain in his side and eased back down. "Whose bloody grave?"

"The Reverend Charles L. Dodgson, better known as Lewis Carroll. He was buried in Guildford in 1898."

"Why do you think that I had anything to with that?"

"The money in that envelope—all but one £20 note—was paid as ransom for the return of some bones removed from the grave. We have a list of the serial numbers and most of them match."

"Are you serious?"

"Quite serious."

"Look, I didn't do it," George protested.

"The evidence suggests that you probably did."

"I can see that it looks bad, but I'll tell you what really happened and how I came by the money."

"Are you aware that having already lied to me is a serious offence?"

"It ca'n't be as bad as robbing Lewis Carroll's grave! I'll tell you what happened. The truth."

"Do you wish to have your solicitor present?"

"No, I'll just tell the truth. Yesterday this little bloke came in and said that there should be an envelope waiting for collection. Said it would be addressed to his wife, Dinah. He told me it contained some embarrassing snaps that he didn't want her to see. He gave me a twenty to drop the envelope in the trash so he could collect it out there. I got to thinking and decided that the envelope might have more in it than a few dirty pictures, so I tore open a corner and saw the money. I decided it was probably drug money or something, and that I needed it worse than he did. So, I took the money out and stuffed the smaller envelope it was in into one of the arms of my jacket. It was too much to fit in my pocket. Today, as I was tossing the trash into the bin someone snuck up behind me and tapped me on the shoulder. When I turned he punched me in the jaw. It must have been the same guy that gave me the twenty, but it's hard for me to understand. He was just this scrawny little guy with bad teeth. He sure had one hell of a punch!"

"Perhaps he was a martial arts expert," DI Spectre suggested. "If he was, then you might well be lucky to be alive. Or it might have been an accomplice. What you've told me this time lines up with the basic facts of the ransom as we know it, so I believe you. I'm confiscating the money as evidence. It's not your money in any event. Nonetheless, PC Eggleton will give you a receipt. I will discuss the particulars of this interview with my superiors to see if they wish to lay charges of obstruction of justice and larceny against you. They may. I can not make any promises in that regard. We will be in touch. In the future, Mr Bander, I would suggest that the best thing to do is tell the truth when discussing anything with the police."

"I promise," he assured him. "It was just a lot of money and I was sure that it wasn't really his, so I was tempted beyond what I could bear. I realize that this was a very serious mistake on my part."

"Could you identify the man who gave you the twenty if you ever saw him again?"

"No problem. He looked like a weasel with crooked teeth."

"Good. We may need for you to do that someday. We will see ourselves out."

They left and as they were walking back down the hallway they could hear Mrs Bander throwing all four bolts.

Spectre turned to PC Eggleton. "Be careful handling the £20 note. It may have the fingerprints of the weasel we're looking for on it. Send it off for analysis as soon as we get back."

"How did you know that he was lying?" PC Eggleton asked.

"When he told us that he worked at the White Hart and that he had gotten assaulted the next day after the ransom was paid. I suspect that our anonymous tip came from the same little weasel we are looking for. He probably wanted revenge for having been ripped off."

When they returned to headquarters Spectre arranged for himself and PC Eggleton to view the CCTV tapes to see if they could spot a small man with horrible teeth talking with George Bander.

"Run the tape at fast speed, Jack, starting at opening time," he told the technician, "until I tell you to stop."

The tape ran for a few minutes.

"Stop!" Spectre said. "That's Mr Richards delivering the money." He pointed to a man on the monitor. They watched him briefly talking to the manager, handing him the envelope, and then leaving. "Fast forward, please, Jack." The tape ran until a crowd began to build as lunchtime approached. "Stop! Please run the tape at real time speed from here, Jack." They watched until they spotted a small man wearing a wide brimmed hat step up to the bar and talk with Bander. "Stop! Run it back a few minutes, Jack, then slow it down. They watched closely as Brian came in. "There's our man," Spectre said. "Blast! He's wearing a hat!" They watched as Brian chatted with Bander, and then left. "Waste of time, I'm afraid," Spectre said, "what with him wearing that blasted hat! You ca'n't see his face. He's shrewd, I'll give him that. Probably guessed we might have a camera aimed at the bar. Nonetheless, Jack, save this tape as evidence. You can erase the rest of them. Send someone over to the White Hart and retrieve the CCTV."

CHAPTER X

Reporting

pectre rang Mark Richards. "Hello," Richards said as he answered.

"Mr Richards?"

"Speaking."

"Good day. This is Detective Inspector Ian Spectre. I wanted to bring you up to date."

"Ahh! Yes. Good of you to call, Detective Inspector. We have been wondering what has happened. I delivered the money to the White Hart, as instructed."

"Yes. Unfortunately, the money was stolen by one of the bartenders, a Mr Bander, who decided to keep it for himself. So our grave-robbers never got it."

"Oh, dear. The Estate is going to be furious!"

"There's some good news and bad news here. Mr Bander was assaulted the next day and seriously injured. We are going on the theory that he was attacked by the person who had expected to receive the money."

"Will he be all right?"

"He's at home nursing a concussion and some broken ribs, but he will survive. The good news is that we have recovered the ransom money. The bad news is also that we have recovered the ransom money."

"Ahh! You've begun asking riddles, Inspector! How did you find out that Mr Bander had the money?"

"We received his name and address from someone who phoned in an anonymous tip. We suspect it was the person who assaulted him."

"I say!"

"The bad news is that the person who has Mr Dodgson's bones is going to be very unhappy at having missed the ransom payment."

"Yes, I can see that. So, Inspector what do we do now?"

"Not much we can do except to wait and see if you receive a new ransom note. They—I am assuming that there is more than one person involved in this—may increase the amount they now want in return for the bones."

"I hope not! The Dodgson Estate was very firm on this point. They will refuse to provide more than the £500 they already have."

"Perhaps the Lewis Carroll Society might be willing to make up the difference," Spectre suggested.

"Perhaps, as long as it is a modest sum. How much might that be?"

"A few hundred pounds; maybe less."

"I will have to ask them. They might prefer to make a special appeal to the Society's membership."

"We can wait until we know the exact amount—assuming that they decide to contact you again. I suspect that they will. The problem with the idea of a public appeal to the Society's membership is that you will no longer be able to keep the public from knowing what's up."

"What will happen to our Mr Bander?"

"I'm not sure, but I suspect that some charges will be laid. Since he has cooperated and the money has been recovered, that will mitigate things a bit. Perhaps a few months in prison or a fine."

"It's very unfortunate that Mr Bander got in the middle of this!"

"Yes; most unfortunate. For him *and* us! Please let me know if you receive another ransom note."

"Yes, of course. I will ring you immediately."

"Good-bye, then, Mr Richards."

"Cheerio."

An hour later PC Eggleton knocked on the door to DI Spectre's office. "Come in!" he said with a loud voice.

PC Eggleton opened the door and stepped inside. "Excuse me, Guv. I just wanted to tell you that we have the results back on the fingerprint analysis on the £20 note that we confiscated from Mr Bander."

"What have they found?"

"As you would expect, there are numerous prints, since it's an old note. Most unidentifiable, I'm afraid. However, they found a match for two men based on the prints in the UK database. One has been in prison for the last six moths and is still there, so we can safely rule him out. The other one is a Brian Mome. He has a bedsit in Putney. He's been arrested three times for petty theft. Nothing more serious."

"Excellent, PC Eggleton! Put him under surveillance. Don't spook him. I don't want him to know that we are watching him. Get me a print of his mug shot, will you?"

"Yes, Sir. Right away, Sir."

Meanwhile, over in Putney, Brian and Toby were sitting on the edge of Brian's bed trying to figure out what to do next.

"Perhaps we should just abandon the bones and try to flog the books," Toby suggested.

"No, we have to do this right to get the big payoff. I'll send another demand note. Give them a bit of a squeeze for a little more money this time, to pay for our troubles."

They both sat silently for awhile as Brian's brain churned, trying to figure how to pick up the ransom without getting caught.

CHAPTER **XI**

Increasing

Mark Richards discovered the new ransom note in the mail two days later.

NO MORE FREE FINGERS. LEAVE £750 IN OLD UNMARKED TENNERS IN AN ENVELOPE AT THE FRONT DESK OF THE IBERIA VICTORIA 20 DEC. WRITE: "FOR COLLECTION—DINAH" ON IT. THIS IS YOUR LAST CHANCE. ANOTHER SCREW UP WE SMASH THE BONES TO BITS AND SCATTER THEM ALL OVER LONDON.

Richards immediately rang DI Spectre and left a short message that the new ransom note had arrived. Twenty minutes later DI Spectre knocked on Richards' front door. "Do come in, Detective Inspector."

"Mr Richards, nice to see you again."

"And you, Inspector. The ransom note's on the desk in my office. Just follow me."

Spectre read the ransom note. "As I expected, the price has gone up, not that it's any of your doing. I'll take this on back

68

to The Office. Please see if you can arrange for another £250."
He reached into his coat pocket and produced the original
£500, which he handed to Richards.

"I will ring the Dodgson Estate immediately after you leave
and see if they are receptive to that idea. As I said earlier, I
doubt that they will be."

"How do you suppose the Estate and Society would react to
the threat of smashing the bones and scattering them?"

"They would be devastated; no, 'horrified' would be a better
word. How could these scum even think of doing such a
thing?"

"They obviously lack any morals or conscience, and only
regard themselves. I suspect that they might well be capable
of almost anything."

"Even murder?"

"Anything."

"Well, I hope that things will work out better this time."

"Give me a ring later, when you know if you will be able to
raise the additional money."

"Detective Inspector, I promise you that we will have the
money. If necessary I will provide the balance out of my own
funds."

"Really?"

"Indeed. I am a great admirer of Mr Dodgson. I certainly
want to see his remains properly buried again."

"Very well, I shall leave it in your hands."

"Need I remind you that the Estate still expects you not to
interfere in the transaction? As the note says, this is our last
chance to recover the bones."

"Yes, I understand. However, once you have retrieved the
remains I shall do everything in my power to arrest whoever
is behind this. With any luck, we may even be able to recover
the ransom, but I don't want you to get your hopes up of that
happening."

"I quite realize that there is the risk of its loss. I am willing to accept that risk for a happy outcome to this very unhappy situation."

"Very well, I'll say good-bye then."

Richards immediately rang the Estate, but they were not receptive to providing additional money. Richards went to his bank and withdrew £250 in £10 notes.

CHAPTER **XII**

Collecting

On 20 December Mark Richards delivered the envelope to the front desk of the Iberia Hotel, a budget hotel about six blocks from Victoria Station.

"May I help you?" an attractive Spanish-looking young woman at the desk asked him.

"Yes, I would like to leave an envelope here at the front desk if I may. A man will collect it later today. You will know who it is when he mentions the name Dinah, which is, as you can see, written on the envelope."

"Is he a guest at the hotel?"

"I don't know." Richards decided to lie. "I believe that he intends to meet one of your guests here this afternoon in the lobby."

"Which guest? I will call and confirm it."

"He didn't tell me."

"Then I'm sorry, Sir. I ca'n't accept an envelope unless he is a guest at the hotel. That's the hotel's policy."

Richards panicked. "Could I please speak with the manager?"

"Of course. Just a moment and I will get Mr Santiago for you."

A few moments later a man emerged from an office behind the front desk. "May I be of the helps, Sir?" the manager asked in a strong Spanish accent. "My name is Santiago. I am the Day Manager."

"I would like to leave this envelope at your front desk for collection. This young lady tells me that this is against your hotel's policies."

"She is the corrects, absolutely. For all we can know it might contains the bombs or the weapons of mass destructions. We can not accept the big risks, since it might be dangerous for our employees and the valuable guests who might be getting the injuries or even dead. It is possible. No, Sir, I cannot allow it!"

"Just a moment, Mr Santiago, while I ring the police." Richards took his cell phone out of his jacket pocket and rang Spectre. "Detective Inspector Spectre, this is Mark Richards.

I'm at the Iberia. We have a problem. The hotel management will not allow me to leave the envelope at the front desk. What should I do?"

"Please let me speak to the manager."

Richards handed his cell phone to Santiago. "DI Spectre would like to speak with you."

"Yes?" the manager asked in a haughty tone into the cell phone.

"This is Detective Inspector Ian Spectre of the Metropolitan Police Service. It is most important to us that you allow someone to pick up this envelope."

"How do I have the knowledges that you are who you say you are?" the manager demanded. "For all I know you could be the terrorist!"

"I will come down and show you my credentials. I should be there in approximately 15 minutes at the latest."

The manager handed the cell phone back to Richards. "He says he will come here and show me his badges. Perhaps you would like to take the seat. We will wait for him to show us his face. Take the envelope with you and keeps it away from the front desk. I don't want to risk it blowing up with the loud boom on one of my guests doing the check in. Go!"

Richards had little choice, so he went over and took a seat.

It only took Spectre ten minutes to get to the Iberia. He walked directly over to the front desk and asked to see the manager. When Santiago reappeared Spectre held up his credentials so that Santiago could see them. "I am Detective Inspector Ian Spectre." He motioned to Richards to join them. "Can we speak to you in private?"

"Of course. Follow me and we can do the private talking in my office." The manager led the way. Once they were in his office he closed the door. "Now, what are the problem?"

"I would very much appreciate your cooperating with the police in this matter. A very old person is in grave danger if a man shows up here to collect the ransom that is in that 'for-collection' envelope and it is not here."

"Oh, really?" he asked with a sceptical tone to his voice. "Exactly what sort of danger?"

"There is a serious threat to smash his skull into tiny bits and spread them all over London if anything goes wrong with his attempt to pick up this envelope which contains a ransom. Could you live with that on your conscience?"

"Holy Mother of Jesus! Are you serious?"

"Quite serious. Is it really asking too much for you to cooperate to prevent that from happening?"

"No, of course not! It is my duty to civics. Please, give me the envelope. I will personally see that this horrible man gets it." He turned to Richards and asked, "Is this ransom for a relative?"

"No, but it is for someone very dear to my heart, I can assure you."

"Don't worries. I shall be sure that he get it!"

"Don't confront whoever asks for the envelope," Spectre cautioned him "He may be dangerous. Just give him the envelope and allow him to leave."

"Of course! I shall be as polite as I can. Should I offer him the cup of coffee?"

"No, I wouldn't do that. Just give him the envelope. Say nothing. Smile if you want to. Let him leave."

"Okay, okay. Now I understand completely now. Would you like for me to takes his picture with my cell phone?"

"No. I definitely would not do that! Believe me, he may be dangerous!"

"Oh! Yes, I see, no, I sha'n't be taking the photographs then! No coffee; no photographs. Yes, I got it!"

"Good. Thank you for your cooperation," Spectre said and offered his hand, which the manager took and shook too vigorously.

"Not at all!" the manager said and then bowed slightly, as if he thought Spectre was Japanese. "It is the very least things that I can do!"

"Thank you. We need to leave now."

"Yes, of course!" The manager reached over and opened the door for them. "I hope that your dear friend's skull will not be bashed to the pieces," he said to Richards as he passed by.

Spectre and Richards walked out together. "The man is an idiot!" Spectre said, shaking his head. "Can I give you a ride somewhere, Mr Richards?"

"No, that's not necessary. I'll just pop over to Victoria Station and connect with the Tube."

"I hope that our suspect didn't see us talking with the manager," Spectre said.

An hour later Brian entered the lobby, wearing a cheap wig and an obviously false moustache. He went up to the desk and spoke to the girl at the counter. "I am here to collect an envelope addressed to Dinah."

"Of course. Just a moment while I ring for the manager. He has it in his office for safe keeping—Mr Santiago, there is a man here at the front desk asking to collect an envelope for someone named Dinah."

Santiago rushed out of his office, envelope in hand, which he thrust at Brian. "I'm very sorry, Sir, but we have no coffee this morning."

Brian took the envelope and gave Santiago a quizzical look, before turning to leave through the front doors.

Toby, who had been patiently sitting in the lobby by the wall where there was a fire alarm box, reached over and pulled the lever, before quickly following Brian out the front door. After a brief delay, by which time they had walked out onto the paving, the alarm engaged and chaos erupted inside the lobby as the fire water sprinkler system was tripped and fire alarms annunciated. On their way to Victoria Station Brian stopped and had a quick peek inside the envelope, and was relieved to see that it was filled with tenners. As they entered the station they went into the loo and removed their wigs, tossing them into a waste bin as they left.

Half an hour later Brian and Toby were enjoying a Fosters at The Kangaroo and Didgeridoo a few blocks off of Piccadilly Circus. "Where shall we leave the bones then?" Toby asked, anxious to be rid of them.

"I've been giving that a lot of thought. Tomorrow we'll take the box to the London Zoo and leave it somewhere. Eventually someone will notice it and take it to lost and found. I'll call in an anonymous tip to the Police to tell them where they can pick it up."

"So, are we still going to go into the used book business then?"

"I've been thinking that over as well and I think that it has too many problems."

"What then?"

"I'm thinking it would be better to visit the bookshops in Hay-on-Wye. We'll spend the night in a hotel to prove that we were there. We'll go from shop to shop until we find a box of cheap books for sale out on the sidewalk, which we'll buy and ask for a receipt. We'll claim that the old *Alice* and the diary were in the bottom of the box."

"Where's Hay-on-Wye?"

"On the border between England and Wales."

"You want to go all the way to Wales to buy a box of cheap books?"

"Yeah. Look, you don't have to go if you don't want to. I'll go alone in the van. I know the area. I have an uncle what lives near there. I used to visit him sometimes in the summer."

Toby shook his head. "You've gone barmy!"

"No I haven't. There's a good chance that some of the ransom money we got is marked. I'll take it along and use it to buy little things here and there. The change I get back will be clean. I don't think it's safe to spend any of it here in London. Sooner or later it will turn up and the police will be on our trail."

"OK. But I'm passin on taking the scenic tour of Wales. When are you leaving?"

"Right after we drop off the bones at the zoo."

They finished their beer and took the tube back to Putney. They went up to Brian's bedsit, where he picked up a suitcase he had already packed. "Where's the books?" Toby asked.

"Here in this case. We don't dare leave them here while I go away for a few days. Someone could break in a steal them. I'll take 'em with me, so I can watch them. Let's go on down to the garage."

When they reversed the van they heard something rolling around in the back. Brain stopped the car and Toby got out to have a look. When he opened van door he jumped back. Dodgson's skull was sitting there on the bare metal deck of the van staring at him. Tobey slammed the door then ran over to

Brian's window. "The bloody skull's out of the box again! That's what was rollin around!"

"No way!"

"Yes! I've just seen it! It's alive, I tell you!"

No sooner had he said this they could hear the skull rolling around inside the back of the van again, banging into the metal sides.

"You'd better get the van back into the garage!" Toby said. "We've got to get that bloody thing back in the box! We ca'n't go driving away with it loose back there! What if it decides to tear our throats out?"

"It ca'n't," `Brian said. "It's got no mandible."

"No what?"

"Mandible. No lower jaw. So it ca'n't bite." Brian put the van in gear and pulled back into the garage and got out. "Now what?" he asked.

"We could open the door and let it roll out onto the street!" Toby suggested, trying to be helpful.

"That's daft! I'm not chasin a skull down the street like a bloody football!"

Toby shrugged. Suddenly the banging noises in the van went silent. Toby and Brian looked at each other, not knowing what to do. "Maybe it went back inside the box," Toby suggested.

"The bloody box is taped up!"

"So what? It got out didn't it?"

"I'll take a look," Brian said and opened the van door a crack, just wide enough to peek inside, but not big enough for the skull to escape. "There's no skull!"

"What do you mean there's no skull?"

Brian opened the door wide. "I think you must be hallucinating, Toby. I've not seen the skull yet!"

"You've heard it!"

"Yeah, I've heard something what sound like it rolling around in the back, but I've seen no skull!"

"It must have gone back inside the box."

"Don't be daft. It's wrapped up tight. The tape hasn't been cut!"

"I don't care. Somehow it's back in the box. I'll wager a fiver on it."

"I'll take the bet. I'll go get a box cutter and a roll of packing tape and we'll look inside the box. You stay here and watch the van. I'll be back in a few minutes." Brian charged off. When he got back they cautiously opened the box. The skull was indeed back in the box. "This is too bloody weird!" Toby said. "We need to get rid of these bones! Let's head for the zoo right now! The sooner the better! And you owe me a fiver."

Brian paid up.

An hour later they bought entrance tickets and walked around until they came upon the bighorn sheep exhibit. All of the sheep were asleep inside their pen. It was so boring that there was no one around. They tossed the box into the sheep paddock and left.

CHAPTER **XIII**

Exploding

After closing, Zoo Security performed their routine walk-through to be sure everyone had left before locking up for the night. While making their rounds one of them spotted the box containing Mr Dodgson's bones lying in the bighorn sheep enclosure. The big ram had also noticed it and was staring stupidly at it. Worried that the cardboard

box, heavily wrapped in packing tape, looked like a bomb, he ran over behind a concrete wall for shelter in case the ram was to butt it and set it off, and radioed the main Security office to call in a bomb alert.

The Bomb Squad arrived 20-minutes later. A man wearing a heavy bomb disposal suit investigated the box and decided that it did indeed look very suspicious, especially since at the moment it was literally vibrating, as if there was something mechanical or alive inside. A zookeeper entered the enclosure and chased the ram back into its pen, and once the sheep were safe a robot was used to plant a small sticky explosive charge on top of the box that was now bouncing around in the dirt as if there was a live wallaby inside trying to get out. A few minutes later the bones were literally blown to bits.

Brian waited for two hours after the Zoo closing time to call Crimestoppers again. He spoke into the recorder, "The police can pick up Dodgson's bones at the London Zoo lost-and-found. They're in a cardboard box wrapped in packing tape."

A few minutes later PC Eggleton burst into DI Spectre's office. "Sir, we've just had a message from Crimestoppers that Mr Dodgson's bones were left in a cardboard box at the London Zoo. As it happens, the Bomb Squad blew up a suspicious-looking cardboard box about and hour-and-a-half ago. There's a pretty good chance it was Mr Dodgson's bones."

"Blast!" DI Spectre said.

"Exactly," PC Eggleton said.

Spectre rang the Bomb Squad dispatcher and told them to secure the area and bring in personnel to recover bone fragments. Then he and PC Eggleton drove over to the zoo to see for themselves. By the time they arrived there were no less than ten Metro Police vehicles parked at odd angles in front of the entrance. DI Spectre and PC Eggleton showed their identification to the PC guarding the entrance gate. "Where was the package blown up?" Spectre asked.

"Good evening, Sir. I understand it was in the Ungulates. Here's a guide map that may be of use." He handed Spectre one of the colourful quad-fold brochures that are handed out to zoo visitors when they buy their entrance tickets.

In another five minutes Spectre and Eggleton were at the blast site and Spectre located a sergeant who seemed to be in charge. "DI Spectre," he told him. "Are you aware that the box that was blow up contained Lewis Carroll's bones?"

"Yes, Sir. So I've been told. Very unfortunate, I'm sure."

"Very."

"All the King's men and all the King's horses ca'n't put them back together again, Guv."

PC Eggleton had to stifle a snicker. Normally DI Spectre had a good sense of humour, but in the present circumstances it had left him. "Now is a very poor time for humour, Sergeant!" he barked. "A ransom for the safe return of the bones was paid earlier today. Get some men in here immediately and start collecting fragments so they can be returned to his family for reburial. Get some bright lights brought in here so you can see what you're doing! Search around the area of the blast for at least a 50-meter radius. Warn your men to be careful climbing into pens and paddocks. We don't want any of them bitten, gored or trampled!"

"Sir!" the Sergeant said. "Yes, Sir!" He scurried off like an ungulate chased by a hyena.

"What a mess!" Spectre said to PC Eggleton.

"Yes, Sir!" He started to tell an omelet joke then wisely decided against it.

Recovery efforts continued through most of the night. Bits of skull cap were found in the nearby okapi pen and several teeth in the kudu paddock. Still more teeth had been carried all the way over into the mountain goat habitat, where they had been difficult to find in the faux rocks and crags. By the end of the night the search team had recovered twelve teeth (which seemed to be blast-resistant) and 56 other fragments in sizes varying from the size of a pea to one fragment about the size of a 20p coin. One of the two phalanges had landed across the way in the polar bear enclosure where it could be clearly seen, but no one was brave or foolish enough to go in and retrieve it. When zoo personnel finally got the bears safely into their cages they discovered that the bone had evidently provided one of the two bears with a small nighttime snack.

About sunrise the sergeant came up to DI Spectre and handed him a polythene bag containing the bone fragments and teeth. "This is all we have been able to find, Guv. I think it accounts for all of the bigger pieces. The rest is indistinguishable powder."

Spectre nodded. "Thank you, Sergeant. Pack up and dismiss your men. File a report when you get back to The Office."

A few hours later Spectre rang Richards, who was busy eating a disgusting, very runny poached egg and dry toast. "Mr Richards, this is Detective Inspector Ian Spectre. Did I wake you?"

"Good morning, Inspector. No, you didn't wake me. I'm in the middle of eating a light breakfast. Been up for an hour, actually."

"Have you heard anything about a suspected bomb being blown up by the Bomb Squad at the London Zoo last evening?" he asked.

"No. Why do you ask?"

"It's a long story, so I wo'n't give you all of the details. In summary, we received a tip that a box containing Mr Dodgson's bones had been abandoned in the London Zoo. Unfortunately, Zoo Security discovered the box several hours earlier and thought it might be a bomb, so they called in the Bomb Squad. The Bomb Squad knew nothing about the bones and as a precaution they blew up the box."

"Oh, Lord! Don't tell me this is true!"

"Sadly, Mr Richards, it is indeed quite true. We had a team of twenty constables scouring the zoo grounds in the vicinity of the blast all night and they managed to recover a dozen teeth, along with 56 other bone fragments, the largest of which is a fragment of the skull cap. I could also identify a small fragment of one of the orbits, but the rest are pretty badly damaged beyond recognition by anyone other than a pathologist. I'm sad to report that a polar bear evidently ate one of the finger bones"

"Really? A polar bear?"

"Yes. Unfortunately it landed in their enclosure and by the time they had chased the bears back into their cages it was too late to go in an retrieve it."

"How odd to think of one of Mr Dodgson's bones in the stomach of a polar bear!"

"Perhaps it would be best not to tell the Estate. Anyway, I would like one of my men to bring the fragments by your home today after we finish photographing them, if that would be acceptable. I assume that the Estate will want to rebury them as soon as possible."

"Of course."

"What time would be good for you?"

"How about one o'clock?"

"That will be fine. That will give us plenty of time to get the photographs taken."

Spectre rang off and Richards immediately rang the Estate to explain what had happened and to make arrangements to send them the remains. He took the DI's advice and didn't tell them about the polar bear. There was enough screaming and crying on the other end of the line as it was when they heard the bad news.

A few minutes later Spectre got hold of the detectives who were assigned to the Mome surveillance team. "This is DI Spectre. What can you tell me about Mome's whereabouts yesterday and at present?"

"We followed Mr Mome over to the location of a garage that he leases to park his van in. He and another man, whom we haven't yet identified, were observed acting very strangely."

"How do you mean?"

"Well, Mome backed his van half-way out and then suddenly stopped and they both bolted, as if they had discovered a snake in the vehicle with them. At one point Mome ran back inside his bedsit and returned with what looked like a box cutter and some packing tape. They were screaming and running around the van like idiots and then they suddenly jumped back in the van and took off at high speed. We tried to follow, but lost them in traffic. No idea where they went after that. Sorry, Guv."

"Put a rush on identifying the other man. He may have been an accomplice in the grave-robbery."

"We took a few telephoto shots of him as well as videotaping the entire episode. If he has a driving licence we will know who he is shortly. The film is being processed as we speak."

"Call me when you know who he is. Get search warrants for his and Mome's residences. Call me when you're ready to move in. I will join you."

"Yes, Sir, we're on it."

CHAPTER **XIV**

Dating

Not surprisingly, with so many people involved, the Bomb Squad's activities at the London Zoo had been leaked to the tabloids and they were once again in full cry, even though details were sketchy and contradictory. Tuck Nipp had been anxiously watching the tabloids for weeks for any news about what might have happened to Mr Dodgson's skull. Once again, he first read the news in the *Natural Inquisitor*:

LEWIS CARROLL'S SKULL BLOWN TO BITS
BY BOMB SQUAD IN LONDON ZOO!
HUGE RANSOM REPORTEDLY PAID BY LEWIS CARROLL
SOCIETY AND MR DODGSON'S ESTATE.
POLAR BEARS UNHARMED.

Tuck grabbed six copies for his collection and for his semi-normal Carrollian friends, then rushed out to his pickup in the Wal-Mart parking lot to read the details about what had happened.

Sources close to the investigation, who wish to remain anonymous because they are not authorized to speak to the media, have given *NI* the following account of what went wrong last night in the London Zoo. As has been widely reported, the skull and several finger bones were stolen from the grave of the Rev. C. L. Dodgson, better known to the world by his pen-name of Lewis Carroll, last October 31 in Guildford, Surrey, UK. These sources believe that a ransom of £75,000 was paid by the fabulously wealthy Dodgson Literary Estate and the Lewis Carroll Society for the safe return of the bones for proper Christian reburial. The bones, which were in a cardboard box, were abandoned in the London Zoo inside the polar bear enclosure, where they were spotted by Zoo Security, who thought that the suspicious box containing the bones might be a bomb and called in the Bomb Squad, who blew it up as a precaution. The noise of the blast reportedly frightened a wildebeest in a nearby pen so badly that it smashed headlong into a wall and died instantly from a broken neck.

A thorough search of the area was finally conducted after Zookeepers shot the polar bears with tranquilizer darts and were able to safely enter their filthy enclosure. A total of 560 tiny fragments, most of the teeth and the top of the cranium were recovered.

Mr Mark Richards, longtime Chairman of the secretive Lewis Carroll Society, had reportedly been working undercover with the police in attempting to recover the bones and was reportedly the one who delivered the ransom to the Iberia Hotel where it was picked up by one of the criminals. Repeated calls to Mr Richards' home phone have not been returned and he is steadfastly refusing to talk with members of the media.

Detective Inspector Ian Spectre of the Metropolitan Police Service, who is in charge of the case, has issued the following statement: "We regret that our efforts to recover the Rev. C. L. Dodgson's bones intact were thwarted. However, numerous bone fragments have been recovered and returned to the Dodgson Estate for reburial. I would like to assure the RSPCA, Green Peace, Save the Whales, The Sierra Club, Ducks

Unlimited, and all of the other environmentalists groups and distraught school children who have expressed great concern for the safety of the polar bears that the bears were never in any danger whatsoever. In spite of some unfounded rumors, no zoo animals were injured in any way. We have several promising leads as to the identities of those responsible for disturbing Mr Dodgson's grave and are vigorously pursuing them." When asked to confirm the amount paid in ransom DI Spectre only replied, "No comment," and then departed.

Mr Julio Alfonso Diego Gonzales de Santiago, the Day Manager of the Iberia Hotel near Victoria Station, has informed the *NI* that he personally handed the ransom over to a man that he believes to be one of the bone-nappers. "The police asked me to be the cooperator in giving the criminal the ransoms. They tolded me that if I didn't not do this that a very old man would have his skull smashed to bits. Of course I was concerned for this old man and agreed. Soon a small man wearing a cheap wig and false moustaches comes into the elegant Iberia Hotel, conveniently close to Victoria Station, and asked for the envelope containing the ransom monies. He was very ugly and had horrible tooths. Horrible! I was quite frightened that he might kill me with a knife or a fork or something sharp, like a screwdriver. However, I worked up my braveries and gave him the money. As soon as he left some idiot pulled the fire alarm and set off the water sprayers in the lobby. We suffered over £15,000 in the severe damages to the lovely furnitures. I am hoping that the Lewis Carroll Society will repay us. It is the leastest thing they can do! I am very dismayed to find out the very old man the police told me about was in fact dead for over a hundred years and they were just talking about his bones! I will never again be able to believe what the polices tolded me! Such lies would never be told by the Policía to a hotel Day Manager in Barcelona! Never!"

Tuck was still engrossed in reading the article when someone banged on his side window, startling him so badly that he honked the horn. He looked into the face of Jada, who was laughing at him. She motioned for him to roll down the window.

"Hey, Nip Tuck! I thought that was you! Did I skeer you?"

"Hello. Jada," he said. "Yes, you did. I was reading this article and wasn't expecting anyone to smash my window in."

"I've been lookin fer you at the Pride, but I haven't seen you yet. You aren't avoidin me are you?"

"No, not you," he assured her. "I've been trying to avoid that big husband of yours!"

"Oh, he ain't my husband no more, so you ain't got to worry bout him at all."

"Did you get a divorce?"

"Naw, I kilt him."

"What!?"

"I kilt him. Bow huntin accident. It was gittin close to dusk and fer some reason he was crawlin around in the bushes. Maybe he dropped somethin. Who knows? Anyway, he was a big guy and I thought he was a bar comin through the woods. I got off a clean shot. Right through the chest. He bled out in less than five minutes."

"Were you arrested?"

"Course not! It wasn't on purpose or anything like thet! Heck I loved him—well, sort of anyways—so I wouldn't of done thet to him, even though he was sort of worthless! 'Bout the only thing he was really good at was changin flat tars and drinkin beer. He did a lot of both."

"I'm sorry to hear about your loss," Tuck said.

"Oh, I'm over hit. Cain't stay all blue and depressed forever. Got to git up an go to work and stuff. I'll find somebody else one of these days. Maybe somebody better. By 'better' I mean richer!" She laughed hard at her own joke.

"How do you define 'rich', if you don't mind my asking?" Tuck was curious if he might qualify. From time to time he had found himself daydreaming about Jada dressed up in a skimpy *Alice in Wonderland* costume.

"Three times the Federal poverty level," she said without hesitation. "I hate dependin on food stamps! They never let you buy what you really want, jest what's in that stoopid little catalog what they give you. Thet's why I'm over here at the Wal-Mart right now. They take food stamps. I need some milk, flour and cheese. Maybe some pasta. You like spaghetti, Nipper?"

"Sure."

"Maybe I'll cook you some, you want me to. Invite you over and all. I make real good spaghetti. Everbody what tastes it says so. I make it with deer meat and sausage. You could maybe bring a nice bottle of wine or a six pack. Maybe a loaf of thet long skinny bread."

"When?"

"Shoot, I don't know. How bout tonight? Unless, of course, you ain't too busy writin books bout dolls."

He smiled. He was very tempted and thought about it for a moment. "I'm not too busy. I'm just not sure I can find your house up Turkey Creek. They don't have any road signs up that holler."

"How you know thet?"

"I drove up there in October to look at the Fall leaves. I noticed that there weren't any numbers on the houses. No street signs either."

"Yeah, thet's right. But shoot! Nobody needs 'em anyway. Everbody what lives up Turkey Crick knows where everbody else lives already. I could meet you down at the highway where the mailboxes are and lead the way the first time so thet you could find hit by yersef the next time you come fer a visit."

"OK. Sounds good. To change the subject, I don't suppose you ever bought an *Alice in Wonderland* costume did you?"

"Matter a fact, Nipper, I did! Got it off eBay two weeks ago. The biddin dropped off after Hall-o-weenie was over. I was wonderin if I might ever see you agin, and if I did I wanted to be ready. It come in last Monday. Fits right good, too! I reckon you might like it jest fine."

"What time will dinner be ready?"

"Can you git there at them mailboxes by six o'clock?"

"Sure. No problem."

"Good."

"What sort of wine do you prefer, Jada?"

"Wet."

He laughed. "I meant what type. Burgundy? Beaujolais? French? German? Australian? Californian?"

"The last bottle I had was from New Jersey. Tell the truth hit tasted kind of like it had turnips in hit, so I'd like somethin different than thet. I like turnip greens OK, if you add a few ramps, but I'm not too keen on drinkin 'em! Why don't you surprise me? Sounds like you know lots more about wine than I do."

"I'll bring a good bottle."

"The heck with the bottle. Bring a good *wine!*"

Tuck laughed again. "There's something else I've been wondering about. Did you ever get around to reading the original version of *Alice's Adventures in Wonderland?*"

"Yes, as a matter of fact, I did. Took me a week, but I managed to git through hit. I was right proud of myself, readin a whole book in jest a week. I ain't never read too many books."

"What did you think of it?"

"I liked it fine. There was lots of little tiny notes here and thar all over the pages, like a Bible, what explained some of the jokes and the words I didn't know. Maybe someday I'll buy me a copy for my own. I had to take the library copy back about a month ago so they wouldn't send me to jail or somethin."

"Oh, I don't think they would do that!"

"You don't know my probation officer! I even so much as hiccup in public she might send me back. She's a real bitch. One of these days she's goin to push me too far and thar might be another huntin accident." She laughed again. She made a sound like an arrow striking something.

Tuck decided to avoid that particular topic of conversation. "By any chance, was the copy you read called *The Annotated Alice*?"

"How'd you know thet?"

"It's famous. I've got several copies. I'll bring a copy for you as a present."

"Really?"

"Absolutely!"

Jada smiled. "That would be right nice of you, Nip Tuck!"

Tuck had never been so happy in his entire life.

CHAPTER XV

Haunting

rian drove all night and arrived in Hereford early the next morning. Along the way he had stopped every chance he had to buy something inexpensive—a Granny Smith, a bag of Seabrook crisps, a bag of Cadbury Rum & Raisin—that sort of thing—and had used a different tenner to pay for each item. By the time he had reached Hereford he had laundered £60, keeping the change in a separate bag.

Exhausted, he stopped at Nutters, a small café, and ordered his usual breakfast: a cuppa Earl Grey, a grilled kidney, and a biscuit. While he was waiting for his order he bought a copy of *The Daily Shriek*, an infamous London tabloid, to see if they had made the news. Unfortunately they had.

**BOMB SQUAD BLOWS UP LEWIS
CARROLL'S SKULL IN TRAGIC ERROR!**
ONLY A FEW BITS RECOVERED: POLICE RED-FACED!
ZIMBABWE THE RHINO SAFE

Brian quickly flipped over to page A-8 and scanned the brief article:

Anonymous sources close to the investigation of the robbing of
Lewis Carroll's grave, a popular gothic tourist attraction in
Guildford, last October have revealed to the *DS* that a £7,500
ransom had been paid for the famous nonsense poet's nicked
skull and fingers. A box containing the bones was left by the
criminals in the London Zoo's rhinoceros paddock, where they
were to be retrieved by the police. However, they were discovered by Zoo Security, who knew nothing of the matter and
mistook the box for a bomb. They called in the Bomb Squad,
afraid that the bomb might go off and injure Zimbabwe, the
Zoo's breeding male northern white rhino, if he happened to
trample it. Zimbabwe is one of the last surviving members of
this dangerously endangered species.

DI Ian Spectre of The Metro Police Service released a statement which, typically, revealed little, and curiously referred to
polar bears. The *DS*'s other sources have revealed that the police
only recovered a tooth and five or six bone fragments.
According to these same sources, the Metro Police have had
two suspects under surveillance and expect to be able to
announce their arrest shortly.

Brian immediately rang Toby, who was still asleep, but finally managed to wake up enough to answer his cell phone. "Yeah?" he grumbled.

"Toby?"

"Yeah. Who is this?"

"It's Brian! Listen, according to the papers the police are on to us! They've had us under surveillance for days. They know who we are!"

"Where are you?" Toby asked, now jolted wide awake.

"Wales. I told you. When the police arrest you—and it sounds like they will—don't tell them anything about the book and the diary! I'm going to hide it where they will never find it. When we get out of we'll get back together, sell them and collect the money. But you have to promise to tell absolutely no one about the books! Do you understand?"

"Even if the police torture me with electrical shock?"

"They wo'n't, Toby! We don't live in Egypt! The police don't know anything about the books. They wo'n't even know enough about them to ask. We'll go to prison for a few years because of the bones, but when we get out we'll soon be rolling in more money than we ever dreamed of."

"How will we find each other once we're out?"

"You know my auntie what lives up north in Grimsby, right?"

"Yeah."

"Contact her when you're out. She'll know where I am. I might even be staying with her until I hear from you. I better ring off now. The police might be monitoring my cell. Good luck in prison. Trust me and we'll be fine."

Brian wolfed down his breakfast and almost choked on a poorly masticated chunk of kidney. Once back in the van he drove down the familiar roads to Coed Fenni-fach in the Brecon Beacons National Park just over the border in Wales, where his Uncle Cadwalader still lived on the old farm where his ancestors had eked out a living for centuries.

It was nearly eight o'clock when Brian drove up to the gate at his uncle's cottage. He got out, opened the gate, drove in, and then got back out to close the gate behind him. There was a thin ribbon of bluish smoke curling up from the ancient kitchen chimney, so he knew his aunt and uncle were stirring about. He went up to the dark-green front door. It was no more that six feet high, built when people were much shorter than they had become. He pulled the lever to ring a bell on the inside. A few minutes later the door swung open and Brian's uncle Cadwalader loomed in the dark hallway.

"Good morning, uncle," Brian said in his most pleasant voice.

"So it's you, is it, Brian?" he grumbled, his breath hanging like fog on the cold air.

"Yes, sir, it is. Could I be coming inside?"

"Depends."

"On what?"

"What you want."

"Nothing, really. I was just driving through the area and decided to come over this was to say hello and see how you and Aunt Afanen are doing. I haven't seen you for almost five years now. Maybe more; I don't recall."

"Whose fault is that, then? We're always here in the same place. It's you that stays away."

"Well, as you know, I live in London, since that's where the jobs are. And it's a long drive from London to Hay-on-Wye. Petrol's gone all pricey, so I ca'n't afford to drop by as often as I'd like."

"Who's there, Caddy?" a woman's voice called from inside the cottage.

"It's Brian, from London. Says he wants to know how we're doing."

Afanen appeared in the doorway and pushed her husband aside. "Well let him in, Caddy! Are you a heathen that lets one of your own kin stand out in the bitter cold?"

Cadwalader grumbled something obscene in Welsh that Brian could not understand and then turned and went back into the kitchen. "Come in, Brian!" Afaden said brightly. "Come in! Never mind Caddy; he got up on the wrong side of his bed this morning. He's been fretting about our sick cow."

Brian stepped inside. The hall was almost as cold as it was outside. "Come into the kitchen, where it's warmer." She led the way, opening the kitchen door briefly to let Brian pass and then closing it quickly once he was inside, to save the warmth.

Cadwalader was sitting at the small table eating some sort of mush from a bowl and drinking tea. He glanced up as they came in, but there was no softness or greeting in his gaze. "Are you hungry, Brian?" Afanen asked. "I can fix you something hot."

"No, thank you, Aunt Afanen. I've had me breakfast in Hereford. I wouldn't be refusing a cuppa, though."

"Of course. Sit yourself there at the table with Caddy. It'll just take me a minute to make it."

"Thank you," Brian said, then eased into the ancient chair opposite his uncle. "So, Uncle Cadwalader, what's wrong with the cow?"

"Pneumonia, I take it. She's struggling to get her breath. The vet's coming to look in on 'er. Probably a waste of time. I figure she'll be dead by late tonight."

"I'm sorry," Brian said. "Perhaps the vet'll be able to save her. The newer antibiotics might be just the thing."

"Mark my words," Cadwalader said, "she'll not see another sunrise. Too bad; she were a good producer."

"I hope you're wrong, but I know that very rarely happens. No one knows their animals like you, uncle."

Afanen sat a cup of tea in front of Brian, and pushed the sugar bowl and a small ceramic jug of milk near his place so that he could fix his tea the way he liked it. "Where are you working, now, Brian?" she asked.

"At the moment I'm not working at all. I was laid off three month ago," he lied. He hadn't had a job in over two years. "Jobs are hard to find right now, what with the economy being so depressed and all."

"So how are you living then?" Cadwalader asked.

"The government provides enough for me to get by until I can find another job."

"I always figured you would be on the dole!" his uncle said. "You never could hold a job for more than a few months."

Brian didn't take the bait, but rather added a little sugar and milk to his tea, stirred it and set the saucer on top of the cup to let it steep. "Well, I have plans to become wealthy, uncle, and someday I may well drive up in a nice new automobile and offer to buy your farm."

This made Cadwalader laugh, and he banged his fist hard on the table, rattling the dishes and silver. "Now that's a good one! You with enough money to buy the farm! And even if you did, what would you do with it? You couldn't farm if your life depended on it!"

"Oh, I wouldn't farm it. I'd turn it into a shop and sell local crafts to the tourists."

This made his uncle laugh loudly again. "Ye Olde Curiosity Shope then, is it?"

"Well, uncle, you can laugh now, but when you're too old to farm any longer and you ca'n't afford the cost of utilities, and feed and antibiotics for your stock, then you might welcome a reasonable offer."

"How will you run a curiosity shop from prison?" he asked. "I figure that that's where you'll be spending most of your life. You're already well down a ways on that slippery path to destruction!"

Suddenly there was a loud banging on the front door, and Brian started like a hart. Talk of prison made him think it was the police, who had somehow tracked him down all the way over onto the Welsh moors. He started to bolt out the back door, then caught himself and forced himself to be still. "That'll be the vet," Afanen said. "I'll see to it." she scurried out of the kitchen, then quickly returned. "He says that he'll meet you in the barn, Caddy."

Cadwalader got up and went over to the rear door, where he slipped on his wellies and a heavy coat before going outside to the barn.

Afanen came over and sat in the chair beside Brian. "Try not to take him to hard, Brian. He doesn't know any other way. Farming's made him as hard as flint in some ways. But he has a tender heart at times. He was embarrassed when you went to prison, and he has a long memory."

"It's OK, Auntie," Brian said. "It's all I expect of him, so there's no surprise and little hurt in what he says to me. I'm sure that I have been a disappointment to many in the family.

I wonder if I could ask something of you? It's partly the reason I drove here today."

"Of course, Brian. What is it?"

"I have two old books that I think are worth a few quid that I would like to leave with you for safe keeping. Would you keep them for me? I don't dare leave them in my room in London because of the crime. They might be stolen while I'm out looking for a job or simply shopping. It's just not safe in London where I have to live."

"Of course I will," she said. "I have an old blanket chest in the bedroom and I'll put them in the bottom and put me clothes on top. I'll put a note on them that says they belong to you and should be returned should anything happen to me."

"That would be great, Auntie! Thank you. It's a load off my mind to know that they'll be safe with you until I can come back and get them. It might be a year or two. I'm not sure when I'll be back."

"Time doesn't matter, Brian. They'll just be in the chest whenever you want them."

"Thank you. I'll get them from the van and be back in a few minutes." He got up and went to retrieve them, then hurried back in out of the cold. He handed them to her. "Just so you know what they are, one's a children's book and the other's an old Victorian diary. Would you like to see them?"

"Of course I would," she said. "I love old books, especially children's books."

Brian unwrapped them, and handed her the diary first. Then he opened the biscuit tin and removed the *Alice*, which he handed to her.

"Why, it's *Alice in Wonderland*!" she cried. "I *do* love this story, even though it's English! Why, I've even got an old Welsh edition in the bedroom, that I read now and then to brighten my day when I get down or things go badly, as they often do on a farm."

"So, you're comfortable with keeping them for me then?"

"Yes. They'll be safe. I promise."

"Don't show them to anyone, will you? I don't want them to come back later and steal them!"

She laughed. "This isn't London, Brian. You needn't be afraid of that! Not here in Wales. This'll be our secret, and no one will know they're there. Not even Caddy."

Brian smiled. "Do you know the auction house called Sotheby's? It's in London. They sell rare paintings and things like that."

"Yes, I've heard of it. Why?"

"In case something happens to me, and I ca'n't come back for the books I want you to take them into Sotheby's and tell them that you want them to auction them for you. You'll be surprised at what they are worth. I want you to keep the money."

"I couldn't do that!"

"I'm only saying that you should do it in case I don't come back. Accidents and bad things happen. So, just in case, you do that. Don't just take the books to one of the bookshops at Hay-on-Wye. You get on the train and you take it to Sotheby's. Do you understand?"

"Yes."

"And when you do, don't tell anyone where you got them. You just say that you've had them in your blanket chest, and you've decided it's time to sell them. Don't even mention my name. Do you understand? It's very important. Don't mention my name."

"All right, Brian, I'll do as you say, but I'm not expecting to hear that anything's happened to you. I expect you to show up back here at my front door one of these days. I'll be looking for you."

"I'll do me best to stay alive. Now I'll be going," he said; "before uncle comes back. I know that I've upset him and I'm sorry. I'll just say my good-byes to you now, until I see you again some day." He stood up to go. "I hope that your cow survives the night."

Afanen stood up and gave him a lingering hug. "Don't worry about the cow. She's getting old, so it's no surprise that's she's taken ill in this frightful cold. She's had a good life and we've had good milk and butter in return. You take care of yourself, Brian. It's been nice to see you again. Try to stay out trouble. Get an honest job and make some good friends. That's the thing."

Brian nodded and then hurried out to open the gate. He drove the van through and then came back to fix the latch. He drove off towards the north and west, along the back roads and high-hedge lanes. He intended to get as far west of London as he could get. He wasn't about to make it easy for the police to find him. As long as he had some ransom money left he would give them a good run.

He stopped late in the afternoon for petrol and bought a copy of *The Times* to see if there was any news about Toby. There was.

LONDON METRO POLICE NAB ONE SUSPECT IN ROBBERY OF LEWIS CARROLL'S GRAVE

Thursday, 25 December 2014

Brian Sibley, Crime Correspondent

London MPS have announced the arrest of one of two suspects that they believe were involved in the shameless disturbance of the grave of the Rev. C. L. Dodgson in Guildford last All Hallows' Eve. As a result of the disturbance the skull and three finger bones were taken and held for ransom. The Dodgson Literary Estate and the Lewis Carroll Society (London) reportedly paid £750 for the bones so that they could be reburied, but their hopes and good intentions were dashed when the MPS Bomb Squad mistakenly blew up the box containing the relics at the London Zoo when Zoo Security mistook the suspicious-looking parcel containing the remains for a bomb. All that was recovered were some teeth and 56 small bone fragments.

The man arrested today has been identified by MPS as Toby Rath, 29, a former semi-professional boxer and currently unemployed resident of Putney. He has been arraigned and charged with vandalism and desecration of a grave, theft of human remains, extortion, resisting arrest, and assault resulting in grievous bodily harm on six police officers. He is presently in jail, unable to make bail, which has been set at £25,000. His accomplice in the deed most foul is Brian Mome, 32, also an unemployed resident of Putney, present whereabouts unknown. However, police across the UK are searching for him and his imminent arrest is expected. Citizens are asked to be on the lookout for Mome, described as a man of slight build, thinning dark brown wavy hair with receding hairline, and distinguished by a tattoo of Lady Gaga on his right forearm and having particularly horrible teeth. He is thought to be driving an old Telecom Maestro van in poor condition. Licence number: LC42 AAW. Police advise the public not to approach the suspect, but rather to contact their local police service. A reward of £100 has been offered by the Lewis Carroll Society of North America for information leading to his arrest.

Realizing that he would probably be captured within hours, Brian headed for the west coast, anxious for one last look at the awesome sight of the rough North Atlantic in winter. He planned to drive to Aberystwyth and from there up to Snowdonia National Park, where one can almost see forever from the top of the mountains. He assumed that it might well be his last breath of freedom for a long time. On a whim, he took a side trip on the A493 along the coast to Aberdyfi to enjoy the view along the bay.

As he was driving along the coastal roadway he suddenly heard, in very clear and life-like sound, a rather high-pitched, yet masculine voice in the back of the van say,

> *"'Twas brillig, and the slithy toves*
> *Did gyre and gimble in the wabe:*
> *All mimsy were the borogoves,*
> *And the mome raths outgrabe."*

Looking in the rearview mirror into the darkness of the back of the van, he shouted, "Who's there? What are you doing in my van?" There was no immediate reply, so he shouted again, "Who's there? Speak up!"

He had no sooner said this than a man suddenly materialized, as out of nothing, in the passenger seat only a matter of inches away. He was rather tall, grey haired and wearing badly deteriorated and ragged Victorian period clothing, including a dirty black coat.

Brian screamed and almost lost control of the van, which swerved back and forth out of his lane as he braked hard and didn't keep his eye on the road. "Who are you?" he said, his voice shrill with fear. All of the hair on the back of his neck and arms was standing up.

"My name is Mr Dodgson."

The van finally came to a stop in the middle of the road.

"What do you want from me?" Brian demanded.

"I'm looking for a sniveling little Mome and a burly Rath that have been outgribing in my grave."

Brian's bladder involuntarily voided. The head of the apparition abruptly changed as the flesh melted away like heated wax, revealing a skull with perfect teeth and two glowing, red eyes. "You're that Mome!"

Brian jerked the driver's side door open and jumped out of the van, just as a car was overtaking him at high speed. The impact sent Brian sailing through the air and over the edge of a cliff into the bay.

CHAPTER XVI

Reaping

Tuck Nipp was sitting at his computer and went on-line to read the UK Edition at the "TimesOnline" web site. He immediately spotted a brief article about the latest developments in the case of Lewis Carroll's grave-robbery.

From *The Times*
Friday, 26 December 2014
Lewis Carroll's grave-robbers found dead
By Anthony Beaverskat
London MPS announced today that both suspects in the robbing of the Rev. C. L. Dodgson's grave in Guildford on October 31 last have died.

Toby Rath, 29, of Putney, had just yesterday been arrested and arraigned. He was being held in HM Prison Belmarsh in South London. He was found early this morning hanged, an apparent suicide. Belmarsh authorities have released a brief statement that says when Mr Rath was placed in a temporary holding cell with five other inmates that he almost immediately got into fights with them and the guards had been forced to remove him to solitary confinement for the safety of the other prisoners.

Rath was a former semi-professional boxer and those in his cell were unable to effectively protect themselves.

Interviews with the other prisoners in his cell, several of whom remain in hospital, indicate that Mr Rath had evidently been hallucinating, seeing something that he described as a skeleton. An autopsy has been ordered to see if there is any evidence of illegal drug use that might explain his suicidal behaviour. An inquest has been scheduled.

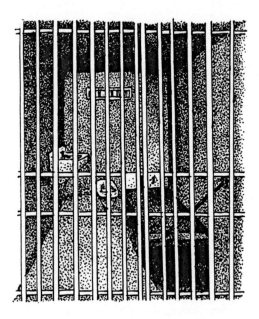

The other suspect, Brian Mome, 32, also of Putney, was the victim of an automobile accident near Aberdyfi on the far west coast of Wales. His van had apparently stalled in the middle of the roadway on the A493 and as an automobile was overtaking his stalled van Mr Mome jumped out and was struck, knocking him over the cliff into the bay. It took police divers more than 13-hours to locate and retrieve his body due to rough seas. No charges have been laid against the driver of the other vehicle, since the accident was judged to have been unavoidable.

"Jada! Come and look at this!"

Jada, who had moved out of her trailer up on Turkey Creek into Tuck's 3,500 square foot, four bedroom, 3 bathroom house in one of the upscale subdivisions in Hurricane, came into Tuck's office to see what he was yelling about. She was wearing a short skirt and high heels, because that was what Nipper liked, and she was determined to keep him happy. "What is it, Nipper, doll?"

"Do you remember me telling you about Lewis Carroll's grave being robbed last Halloween night? And that someone had taken his skull and three finger bones?"

"Of course I do, Honey! That's what we were talkin bout when we first met, thar in the Wal-Mart. How could I ever fergit thet?"

"That's right! Well, the two guys who did it have been found dead. One hanged himself in jail after being arrested. The other one was killed in a car wreck in Wales."

"Where's Wails? I ain't never heard of thet place afore. Sounds a sad sort of name to call a place."

"You've heard of England, of course."

"Sure."

"Well, England is the main country on a large island known today as the United Kingdom."

"Yeah, I know thet, too."

"Good! Well, Wales is part of the United Kingdom, located over on the west side of the island."

"I see. What was thet guy a-doin over thar?"

"I suppose he was trying to run from the police. They were searching for him, because of what he did robbing Lewis Carroll's grave and all. Those two guys managed to make just about everybody in England mad at them for doing that. They made a big mistake in choosing Lewis Carroll's grave for that stupid stunt! Now they've both paid with their lives."

"Yeah," she agreed. "Dumb as dirt, I reckon."

Tuck grinned. He just couldn't get enough of how Jada talked.

CHAPTER XVII

Enquiring

*T*hree months after Brian's visit with his aunt and uncle, Afanen finally learned about Brian's death and what he had done. Naturally it was a big shock and she decided that she wasn't about to be the one to tell Caddy. As a matter of fact, she was hoping that he would never hear about it at all. Finding out that his nephew by marriage was a grave-robber would no doubt infuriate and embarrass him.

As things worked out Afanen never had to tell him, when two weeks later disaster struck when Cadwalader was kicked in the head by their replacement dairy cow. He was in hospital in a coma for a week and then died, leaving her with almost nothing in the bank after paying for funeral expenses. In this desperate financial strait she naturally started thinking about the two books that Brian had left with her for safekeeping and she wondered if Brian's grave-robbing and the books might somehow be related. But there had been no mention in the articles she had read about any stolen books, and so she finally decided that it would be acceptable to sell them. She recalled how Brian had told her that they might be worth a bit of money so she decided to make a few discrete inquiries and see exactly what Brian had left her. So, she rang one of the antiquarian bookshops over in Hay-on-Wye intent on asking a few "what-if" questions without revealing what she had. She chose Boz Books at random.

"Boz Books. Peter Harries speaking. How may I be of assistance?"

"I have a question."

"Of course. I shall try to give you an answer."

"Thank you. I was wondering if a person might happen to have an 1865 edition of *Alice's Adventures in Wonderland* what might it be worth?"

There was a pause. "Are you saying that you have a copy?"

"No, I'm just asking what it might be worth if someone just happened to have one."

"Well, that would depend upon its condition and if it was inscribed by the author to someone famous or important; that sort of thing."

"Well, suppose its condition wasn't too good and it smelled a bit from the damp."

"Even in that condition I would probably be willing to offer the owner £30,000 if it turned out to be a genuine first edition.

It would have to be examined by experts to verify that it wasn't a forgery, of course."

Afanen was silent, too shocked to even know what to say next.

"Hello!" Harries said. "Ma'am, are you still on the line?"

"Did you just say £30,000?"

"Yes. Perhaps more, depending upon the condition of the book."

"I see. I have another question."

"What might that be, then?"

"Suppose, just theoretically speaking, that this same person also happened to have Mr Charles Lutwidge Dodgson's diary starting in 1858. What might *that* be worth?"

Again there was a pause. "Are you saying that you know someone who has it?"

"No, I'm just asking what it might be worth if someone had it—theoretically speaking."

"Well, there would be some problems with selling it. The Dodgson Estate would probably sue to recover it, claiming that it is rightfully their property, since there is no historical evidence that it was ever legally sold. My guess is that they would prevail, since none of his diaries has ever appeared on the market and the ones that are known still remain the property of the Dodgson Literary Estate."

Afanen thought for a moment. "So the owner probably couldn't sell it at an auction, for instance?"

"Probably not. The auction house would regard it as being encumbered."

"Meaning what?"

"Meaning that they wouldn't want to get in the middle of a lawsuit over who legally owned it."

"So, it ca'n't be sold?"

"No, I didn't say that. It would probably be impossible to sell at a public auction, but there are Lewis Carroll collectors who would probably be willing to buy it privately."

"But wouldn't they have the same problem in selling it?

"Yes, if they tried to dispose of it in a public sale they would probably have the same problems. But this might not be an issue, since the buyer might simply want to have it, hold it, and read it. There would be an attraction to having something absolutely unique, even if they could never let the public know that they had it. When they died it might well appear on the market and the Estate might eventually claim and recover it, but the buyer wouldn't care."

"Why not?"

"Why, because he'd be dead."

"Oh! Yes, I see what you mean. Well, suppose the owner wanted to sell it privately to some rich collector somewhere in the world. How would they go about doing it?"

"They would need to go through a third party; someone who knew the names of people who might be interested. The third party would make the arrangements and receive a commission from the seller. It would have to be someone who could be trusted to be absolutely confidential in the transaction."

"And how might a person find such a third party?"

"Well, Madam, as it turns out, you are talking to just such a person."

"But wouldn't this sale be illegal?"

"Technically, it probably would. But if the item is genuine I would be willing to take the risk."

Afanen thought about this for a moment.

"Well, I suppose the bottom line is just how valuable this diary is. Would it be worth the risk to you, personally?"

"Oh, it would certainly be worth the risk."

"You're evading my question. What might it be worth?"

"Well, on the black market—so to speak—it might fetch £100,000. Perhaps even more."

There was silence again as Afanen tried to catch her breath. "That much?"

"Yes. I think that would be a conservative value—to the right person."

"Thank you for your time and advice."

"Wait! Are you—I mean would the owner, whomever they might be—be interested in selling the book and the diary directly to me or to use me as the third party to negotiate its sale?"

"If that should happen then I'm sure that they will know how to get in touch with you."

"How would they know?"

"Why, I'd tell her to contact Mr Harries of Boz Books, of course."

"Thank you, Madam. I hope to hear from her—whomever she might be. Would you mind telling me your name?"

She started to reply and got as far as "Afan—" before she realized that she shouldn't say, and abruptly rang off without saying good-bye.

CHAPTER XVIII

Bargaining

Since she hadn't even read the diary Afanen decided that she should at least do that, to see what all of the fuss was about. She went into the bedroom and retrieved the diary from the blanket chest and read it from cover to cover. When she was finished she still couldn't understand why anyone would be willing to pay so much for it. She wrapped it back up and put it back into the chest while she tried to reach a decision on how best to proceed.

A week later Afanen wrapped up the 1865 *Alice* in a clean dishtowel, put it in her market shopping bag and caught a train to London, where she took a taxi to Sotheby's. She walked up to the reception desk and asked a young woman seated at a desk, "I'd like to talk to the appropriate person for the sale of a very valuable book."

"How valuable do you think it might be, Madame?"

"I have good reason to believe that it is worth at least £30,000."

"I see. Please give me a moment and I'll fetch Mr Stewart. I'm sure that he will want to talk with you about the book.

Please have a seat for just a moment." She gestured to a chair sitting in front of her desk.

A few minutes later a distinguished looking and well-dressed man appeared in the lobby and greeted her. "Good afternoon, Madame," he said and offered his hand. "My name is Lester Stewart."

She shook his hand firmly. "Good afternoon, Mr Stewart. My name is Afanen Dyfnallt."

"It's a pleasure to meet you, Mrs Dyfnallt. How might I be of service?"

"I have a book that is apparently worth a great deal of money and I am considering placing it up for auction. I'd like to discuss how to go about doing that."

"Do you have the book with you?"

"Yes."

"Good. Please come into my office and you can show me the book and we can talk about it after I've seen it. Can I offer you a cup of tea, Mrs Dyfnallt?"

"That would be lovely."

They went into his office, where he offered her an antique chair and rang the receptionist to have someone bring tea. "What sort of book do you have?"

"It's an old children's book." She reached down into her market bag and got the *Alice* which she handed to him. He unwrapped the cloth and instantly recognized the book as an old standard edition of *Alice* from its familiar dark-red cover. He quickly opened it to the title page and when he saw the date his eyebrows shot up. "Why, this is an 1865 edition! My word, Mrs Dyfnallt! If it's genuine it will prove to be a bit of a sensation. We would have to determine if the book is genuine, of course. There are people out there who try to fake this book."

"How would they do that?"

"They would buy an early edition perhaps a fifth or sixth edition worth perhaps a few hundred pounds. They would then replace the title page with a forged one with the 1865 date."

"Would that work?"

"Not with us. We would have an expert examine it. There are fine details that must also be true. An expert could spot them if they aren't correct."

"I see."

"How much do you believe that this book might be worth? I've been lead to believe that it might be worth as much as £30,000."

"How did you come up with that estimate?

"I made an anonymous inquiry with Boz Books in Hay-on-Wye and a Mr Harries offered me that much for it."

"Indeed!"

"To tell you the truth I almost had a heart attack when he told me!"

"I can imagine."

"How did you come to have it?"

"It's been at the bottom of my grandmother's blanket chest in my bedroom."

"And where is that?"

"We live in the family home on a little farm in Wales."

"Where exactly?"

"Near Coed Fenni-fach. It's near Brecon."

"And where might she have acquired it?"

"No one in the family knows."

"We would be very pleased to handle the auction sale of this book. I think that it will easily realize more than double what Boz Books suggested. Perhaps even triple that amount. It's in rather bad condition, but nothing that ca'n't be put right for a few thousand pounds."

"Are you serious?"

"Quite serious."

"Oh, dear!"

"Indeed. As a matter of fact, I'm aware that a similar copy—though in better condition—sold for almost £90,000 in the late 1980s. Once this copy is expertly cleaned up and restored it would be every bit as desirable. What with appreciation and the heightened interest in *Alice* in general, it could very easily command an even higher price. It is a very rare and very desirable book."

"That's very exciting to think about, but I have one worry."

"And what is that, Mrs Dyfnallt."

"Do you have to tell everyone at the auction where it came from? I mean, do you have to reveal my name and where I live?"

"No. We can simply say in the sale catalogue that it is the property of a lady. We will never reveal your name to the public. We will, however, be required to reveal it to Her Majesty's Revenue and Customs for tax purposes, since it is a very valuable book. We will keep this information in strictest confidence."

"What would your fee be? I assume that you will require a little something."

He laughed lightly. "More than 'a little something', I'm afraid. Our fee would be 20 percent of the final hammer price."

She did some quick mental math. "That much?"

"Yes. That is our customary arrangement. We will have considerable expense in handling this. But in return you will have the best chance in the world to find that special person who is willing to pay the maximum amount."

"So it would be money well spent, then?"

"Absolutely! You also might have to pay capital gains tax. You would need to obtain professional tax advice on that matter."

"Tell me, who would you use to examine the book, to be sure that it's genuine?'

"We have a consulting arrangement with Dr Selwyn Goodacre. He is recognized worldwide as the foremost authority on the first editions of *Alice*. He knows all of the finer textual points. If this is a genuine 1865 edition he will soon confirm it."

"I see."

"Well then, Mrs Dyfnallt, shall we go over the details of how to proceed with the sale of your book?"

"Yes, that's why I'm here."

"Good. We have an upcoming sale of rare children's books in March. This would be the perfect venue to offer it for sale. I dare say that we might want to put a colour photograph of it on the cover of the auction catalogue. As it happens, there is also another happy circumstance."

"What might that be?"

"This year is the sesquicentennial anniversary of the publication of *Alice's Adventures in Wonderland*. There are going to be celebrations all over the world about this event and there will be a heightened interest in anything to do with *Alice*, especially the unexpected appearance of a first edition for sale.

I feel confident that when we announce its upcoming sale that it will make headlines round the world."

"Really? Headlines?"

"Indeed. In fact, there will be major exhibitions here in London at various venues, including the British Museum and the Victoria and Albert. The Queen will even be making an appearance at the one at the V&A. You should plan to come and see them. You might even want to consider joining the Lewis Carroll Society and get involved in the events."

"But I don't want them to know that I'm selling the *Alice*."

"Yes, I quite understand. They wo'n't need to know anything about it. You will have the opportunity to meet some very interesting people who know almost everything there is to know about Lewis Carroll. But they certainly wo'n't learn that you were the one who sold this book unless you want to tell them—at least they will never learn of it from Sotheby's, I can assure you of that."

She smiled. "I might enjoy attending a Lewis Carroll Society meeting."

"I'm positive that you would, Madame. They are charming and wonderful people. I've met many of them over the years."

Surprising

$\mathcal{T}$uck first learned of the upcoming sale of the first edition of *Alice* on-line at *The Times* website that he routinely checked every morning.

From *The Times*
Friday, 6 February 2015
Sotheby's to auction rare 1865 *Alice*
By Anthony Beaverskat
Sotheby's announced today the upcoming sale of a rare first edition of *Alice's Adventures in Wonderland* that will be offered at their London auction house on Monday, 9 March 2015, to be included in their upcoming "English Literature, Children's Books and Illustrations" sale as Lot 210. The published catalogue estimate is £90,000-150,000. This may seem trivial compared to the price of a French Impressionist painting, but it is a significant amount for an antique children's book.

This estimated sale price is well below the approximately $US 1.8 million realized for another first edition sold some years ago by New York book dealer Justin Schiller, but that copy was quite unique, having been used by Mr C. L. Dodgson (a.k.a. Lewis

Carroll) as the starting point for an abbreviated version of the story, which Dodgson published as *The Nursery Alice*.

The copy has been examined by Dr Selwyn H. Goodacre, widely acknowledged as the world's foremost authority on the first editions of *Alice's Adventures in Wonderland,* and he has attested to its authenticity.

Nothing is known about the history of this particular copy and the lot is listed in the auction catalogue as simply "The Property of a Lady."

Interest in this particular copy is unusually high since its sale serendipitously coincides with this year's sesquicentennial anniversary of the first publication of *Alice's Adventures in Wonderland*, which will be celebrated with great extravagance and fanfare in numerous locations around the world, including New York City, London, Tokyo, Chicago, Moscow, Paris, and even places as remote as Huntington, West Virginia in the U.S.A.

He was amazed that the small exhibition of materials from his own Carroll collection that he and Jada would curate later this year at the Huntington Museum of Art had actually managed a mention in *The Times*. He hurried into the kitchen where Jada was preparing her famous venison/sausage spaghetti, using the meat from a doe that she had killed with a small hatchet (as a convicted felon she was not allowed to own a gun) during deer season.

"Guess what!" he said. "You wo'n't believe this!"

"What's that, Sugar?"

"Our exhibition at the Huntington Museum is actually mentioned in *The London Times* newspaper! I wonder how in the world they found out about it?"

Jada let out a loud squeal of delight. "Thet's wonderful! I want to see! Just a minute while I sit this pan off the burner."

They rushed back into Tuck's office and he showed her the article. She squealed again and slapped him on the back, leaving a bright red handprint on his shoulder from the force of the blow. Jada just didn't seem to ever realize her own strength. "Congratulations, darlin! I'm sooo proud of you! This is so much fun I cain't hardly stand it!"

"I'll have to call the museum later today and let them know, just in case they don't happen to see it."

"They're a-goin to be real excited, too, I jest know hit!"

CHAPTER XX

Auctioning

At Mr Stewart's suggestion, Afanen contacted the Lewis Carroll Society and found out the details of their next general meeting in London, which she attended. She found the small group of members who attended to be pleasant and friendly, and she greatly enjoyed making their acquaintance. As to the meeting itself, she found it generally over her head, since she was unfamiliar with the rather esoteric topics of the presentations. But she was happy that she had gone and decided that she would attend the next meeting. She was particularly pleased to have met Dr Goodacre, whose name she remembered from her talk with Mr Stewart of Sotheby's.

Naturally Afanen attended the Sotheby's sale. She found a seat and looked around, spotting a few of the Society's members in attendance. Some of them were seated together on a row close to the front and were in obvious high spirits. She recognized Dr Goodacre, Mark Richards, and Edward Wakeling, though she couldn't recall the names of several others that seemed to be in their group. She wondered if they would recognize her.

It was several hours before Lot 210 came up. Bidding started at £20,000 and rapidly rose, with a number of bids coming in by phone. The hammer price was £215,000, well above Sotheby's estimate. It was a result beyond her wildest dreams and hopes. She immediately left the sale room and went to the lobby, hoping that she might see one of the Society members, anxious to hear what they thought of the hammer price.

A few minuets later the man she recognized as Mr Wakeling emerged and she walked over to him. "Excuse me, but aren't you Mr Wakeling?"

"Yes. I'm sorry, but I don't immediately recall your name."

"That's quite understandable. We only met briefly at the last Lewis Carroll Society meeting. My name is Afanen Dyfnallt."

"Of course! I'm so sorry. I should have recognized you. My only excuse is being somewhat distracted by the sale of the 1865 *Alice*."

"Oh, you needn't apologize."

"Did you watch the sale?"

"Oh, yes. I wouldn't have missed it for anything."

"And did you place a bid?"

"No, no! I couldn't have possibly afforded even the opening bid!"

"Nor could I, unfortunately. Still, it was great fun watching the bidding."

"Do you have an 1865 *Alice* in your personal collection, Mr Wakeling?"

He laughed. "No, it is quite beyond my means. First editions of *Alice* are usually only owned by millionaires. However, I do have a great many other wonderful books, so I'm happy. Are you a collector, Mrs Dyfnallt?"

"No, not really, though I do have a first Welsh edition that I enjoy reading, if that counts."

"Of course it does! That is not a common book. So—let's see, your name sounds Welsh and you own a Welsh first edition of *Alice*, which you can *actually* read, so I'll take a wild guess that you just might live in Wales?"

She smiled. "Yes. I live on a small farm in the Brecon Beacons National Park."

"Now, that's a remarkable coincidence. I live just across the Wye, near Hay-on-Wye! Why, we're practically neighbours!"

"Yes."

"In that case, would you be interested in seeing my collection someday? Perhaps you and your husband could drop by on a Sunday afternoon for tea and I will show you more Carroll books than you have ever imagined—maybe even more than you ever want to see!"

"My husband recently passed on, I'm afraid."

"I'm sorry. Please accept my sincere condolences."

"Thank you."

"But you can come by yourself if you would like, or bring along a friend. Please do."

"That would be very nice."

"Wonderful! Shall we make a firm plan? How about Sunday, the 22nd of March at, let's say, three o'clock in the afternoon. Would that be agreeable?"

"Yes. Thank you so much for the invitation. I would love to see your collection."

"Excellent! Let me give you my phone number in case you get lost or need to cancel and my address. I'll draw you a little map so that hopefully you can find me without too much difficulty."

CHAPTER XXI

Exporting

From *The Times*
Tuesday, 10 March 2015
**Rare 1865 *Alice* sold at Sotheby's auction may be
headed for North Korea — or not**
By Anthony Beaverskat
A rare first edition of *Alice's Adventures in Wonderland* was sold
yesterday at auction by Sotheby's (London) for £215,000, well
above the price estimate. The winning bid was placed by Mr Yee
Kar-Lok, a secretive Hong Kong rare book dealer. He has
recently been observed purchasing large numbers of rare and
expensive Lewis Carroll books across the UK. An anonymous
source at the South Korea (ROK) Embassy in London has
indicated that Mr Yee is reputedly acting as a buying agent for
the reclusive Supreme Leader of the Democratic People's
Republic of Korea (North Korea), Kim Jong-un, who is known
to have various expensive Western tastes, including Jean-
Claude van Damme films, pin-ups of Elizabeth Taylor and Julia
Roberts, rare vintage French champagnes, Victorian erotica, and
antique children's books. He has reportedly amassed one of the
largest collections of Lewis Carroll books in Asia, second only to
the vast collection of Yoshiyuki Momma in Japan. Much of his

collection is said to have been inherited from his father, the so-called "Dear Leader" Kim Jong-il.

However, the Great Successor, as Kim Jong-un is known in North Korea, may not get his *Alice* after all, since UK law requires an Open General Export Licence (O.G.E.L.) for any collectors' items over 50-years old and values greater than £180,000. Whether or not the export licence will be granted is unknown. However, several book dealers who have been contacted are of the opinion that the licence will probably be granted, since there are other known copies of the 1865 *Alice* in the UK, and there is nothing particularly unique about this specific copy.

CHAPTER XXII

Withdrawing

From *The Times*
Wednesday, 11 March 2015
**North Korea walks out of Six-party talks in dispute
over export of rare *Alice***
By Anthony Beaverskat
North Korean diplomats have angrily stomped out of a
preliminary meeting for the scheduled session of the stalled Six
Party Talks (China, The United States, North and South Korea,
and Japan) over an apparent hold-up in the granting of an Open
General Export Licence (O.G.E.L.) by the UK for a rare first
edition (1865) of *Alice's Adventures in Wonderland* which was
sold March 10 at Sotheby's (London) to an agent for Kim Jong-
un for £215,000.

Julia Roberts, Assistant Deputy Under-Secretary of State for
North Korean Affairs, has been dispatched to London to discuss
with Prime Minister and comma usage expert Lynn Truss what
might be done to expedite the issue of the O.G.E.L. in hopes of
averting nuclear war on the Korean Peninsula. If the O.G.E.L. is
granted Assistant Deputy Under-Secretary Roberts hopes to be
able to personally deliver the book to the Great Successor, one
of her greatest fans.

CHAPTER **XXIII**

Wakeling

*A*fanen had grown increasingly nervous about having the diary hidden in her bedroom blanket chest, since she was now painfully aware of its potential value, especially to unscrupulous book dealers who might like to sell it to Kim Jong-un. She tried her best to think of some other, more secure place to hide it, but came up with nothing better than the bottom cupboard in her kitchen, behind the pots and pans. She now regretted having ever mentioned the diary to Mr Harries of Boz Books, since he might have somehow managed to figure out that she was the person who sold the 1865 *Alice* at Sotheby's and probably owned the diary as well.

It soon got to the point that Afanen couldn't even peacefully sleep. Every nighttime noise would bring her wide awake as she imagined some North Korean agent had entered the cottage intent on stealing the diary. She even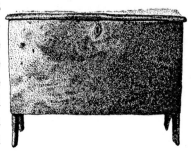

dreamt that there was a North Korean submarine lurking offshore on the west coast, silently waiting for the diary to be delivered by a North Korean frogman so that the prized volume could be whisked away to Pyongyang.

After a week of this sort of torment she finally decided that she had to get rid of the diary. However, she realized that its cultural importance was too great to simply toss into the fireplace. She considered simply sending it to the Dodgson Estate in a parcel without a return address, but then asked herself why would a good Welshman do anything that nice to a bunch of Englishmen? Had not her own Brecon ancestor archers lost their lives fighting for Llywelyn at the Battle of Orewin Bridge? No, it was a matter of personal pride to find something else to do with it.

The Sunday of her planned visit for tea and Carroll collection viewing with Mr Wakeling, at his home near Hay-on-Wye, soon arrived and even though she was groggy from lack of sleep she made her way to his home. She made five wrong turns and arrived fifteen minutes late.

She parked her automobile and walked up to the front door of what she hoped was Mr Wakeling's house. She knocked on the front door and to her immense relief it opened to reveal Mr

Wakeling. "Ah, there you are!" he exclaimed. "I was worried that you had either gotten lost or else those pesky fairies that live hereabout had captured you and drowned you in the River Wye! Come in! Come in!"

"What a lovely home you have, Edward!" she said as she glanced around.

"Thank you."

"I don't believe that I have ever seen so many bookcases outside of a library!"

"Yes, it takes a good many book cases to hold the collection. So, did my map fail you, then?"

"It was an excellent map. The problem is that I'm not an excellent map-reader. I somehow managed to get lost no fewer than five times, but here I am at last! I'm sorry to be so late. It wasn't for lack of trying!"

"It's no problem at all, Afanen! No problem at all. I'm just glad that you're safe!"

They spent the next two hours going from bookcase to bookcase with Edward showing her books that he considered special for one reason or another, telling her how and when he had acquired them. After two hours she was quite overwhelmed by it all and felt exhausted, partly from the lack of sleep, but also because it was simply too much to take in.

"I wonder if we could sit down and rest a minute? I'm quite overwhelmed by everything!"

"Of course! I'm sorry. I get very excited about my books and it never occurs to me that I might be wearing someone out while I am showing them!"

She sat down and smiled weakly.

"Perhaps this would be a good time for tea," he suggested. "Are you hungry?"

"Well, a little bit, yes. I haven't been sleeping too well and I'm feeling a little bit weak because of that. A cup of tea and a biscuit would be lovely."

"Just give me a minute and I'll set the table. I have broiled a nice salmon. And I have some fresh vegetables for a salad, with a lovely raspberry vinaigrette."

"Oh, you shouldn't have gone to such trouble, Edward! I hadn't expected to have a formal dinner."

"This isn't formal at all. We will be quite informal. Catch your breath and I'll just set the dishes."

As they were eating Afanen asked him, "I noticed your name on a few books, so I see that you are an author. What do you mostly write about?"

"Well, Carrollian subjects, as you probably guessed. I have done a good deal of work with Mr Dodgson's photography. He was a Victorian pioneer in that art form and took some of the loveliest early photographs of the Victorian era, perhaps even of all time. I've also spent about fifteen-years of my life editing and annotating Mr Dodgson's diaries. That has been the biggest task that I have undertaken. I keep very busy with numerous projects related to Mr Dodgson's life and work."

"I understand that there are four missing volumes from the diaries," she remarked.

"Yes. You might find it interesting that I undertook to write what might have been two of them. I knew the time period and the people that Mr Dodgson knew and visited often and from various letters and other sources it was possible to reconstruct what he might have written. It was a great challenge and a good deal of fun."

"That's very interesting indeed. Which two volumes did you reconstruct?"

"The first two."

"Which missing volume was the third one?"

"It begins in April of 1858."

"Will you ever try to reconstruct that one as well?"

"Perhaps. I haven't decided just yet."

"Well, Edward, it was really very nice of you to show me a little of your collection. I can see that a person could spend weeks here looking at things and not see it all."

"You're very welcome, Afanen. It's been my pleasure."

"And the salmon was lovely. I have a little gift for you," she said, "by way of a small thank you for my visit."

"Oh, you shouldn't have done that!" he protested.

"It's nothing that you don't already have, but I thought that you might like to have it anyway, as a memory of our afternoon together." She reached into her purse and took out a small present, wrapped in lavender paper decorated with small white flowers and tied with a white bow. "This is with my compliments." she said and she handed it to him.

"Shall I open it now?"

"If you wish," she said and smiled sweetly.

He opened it slowly and carefully so as not to even damage the wrapping paper. "Why, it's a first Welsh edition! Is this the same one that you mentioned to me when we talked in Sotheby's?"

"The same. I have had it for many years, and read it often. I saw that you already had two copies, so I realize that it's not something that will thrill you as much as I had hoped."

"Dear Lady, it is a very generous and lovely gift and I shall always treasure it, since it was from you and because I know the circumstances. It is an extravagant gift."

She beamed. "Well, it's getting late, so I think that I will take my leave." She stood up.

Edward saw her to the door, said good-bye and stood in the doorway waving to her as she drove away.

Wrapping

When Afanen arrived home she knew exactly what she would do with the diary, and it was a great relief to her. For the first time in weeks she slept soundly and woke rested.

The following morning, after fixing herself a bite of breakfast she went and retrieved the diary from the back of the kitchen cupboard. She wrapped it carefully, first in plastic that she cut from a polythene trash bag, to protect it from water damage, then in a clean kitchen towel to protect it from being bumped too hard. Finally she wrapped it in brown paper and placed it inside a cardboard box and stuffed the gaps with wads of newspaper, then sealed it well with packing tape. Satisfied that it might actually survive transport through the post she addressed it and took it to the post office in Brecon where she handed it to the clerk. However, the clerk insisted that the box had to have a return address, so Afanen simply made one up and then handed it back to her.

C H A P T E R **XXV**

Donating

$\mathcal{P}$eter Harries had watched with interest the sale of the 1865 *Alice*, and couldn't help but believe that the unidentified lady who had sold the book was none other than the Welsh woman who had called in February asking him about what such a book might be worth. The more he thought about it the more he also became convinced that she probably also had the missing diary. He recalled that she had started to give her name, but hung up before saying it completely. If he had heard her correctly it was "Afan" something or other.

He finally decided that he might be able to figure out who she was and went on-line to search for Welsh female given names that began with "Afan". He had to check several sites before he found a match, an uncommon old name, Afanen, which meant "raspberry" in Welsh. He assumed that since she had contacted his bookshop that she probably lived in

the immediate area, perhaps in Hay-on-Wye, but more likely across the Wye River, since she had a distinctly Welsh accent.

Harries closed the shop for the afternoon and drove over to Brecon, the nearest town of any size, and went to the Post Office. When it was finally his turn at the counter he asked the clerk, "I wonder if I might speak to the Postmaster? I have an urgent confidential question I need to ask him."

"Just a moment. I'll see if he's available." The clerk went over to a door leading into an office and spoke to someone, then returned to the counter. "He can see you in a few minutes. If you'd please just wait over there he will step out to see you."

"Thank you."

"You're quite welcome. Next!"

Five minutes later a man came out from a locked door. "May I help you?" he asked Harries.

"I hope so. My name is Peter Harries. I'm the proprietor of Boz Books over in Hay-on-Wye." He handed him a business card. "I'm trying to locate someone."

"Please step into my office."

They went inside. "Do you have any identification, Mr Harries?"

"Yes, of course." He showed him his driving licence.

"Thank you. Who are you trying to locate and why?"

"As you can see from my business card, I deal in rare books. I have recently acquired a rare book with an unusual name inscribed in it. It's the Welsh name Afanen. The surname is smudged and illegible. I would like to contact her to see if she can authenticate that she was the previous owner, so that the book will have some provenance."

"You're correct in that it's an unusual name. And a very pretty one, as well. To my knowledge, there is only one woman in this area who has that first name. She occasionally uses this post office. Her married name is Dyfnallt."

"Could you spell that for me?"

"Of course. D-Y-F-N-A-L-L-T. It's a bit difficult to spell, I'll admit."

"Thank you. Can you provide me with her address?"

"I'm sorry, but I'm not allowed to do that."

"If I can provide the book with provenance it will greatly increase its value. It would be worth £50 to me."

"I don't accept bribes, Mr Harries."

"I'm certain that you don't. I wasn't suggesting that. Perhaps I could donate £50 to your favourite local charity in return."

The postmaster thought for a moment. "I am a patron of the RSPCA. If you were to return with a gift receipt that confirms that you made such a payment to them then I would be willing to provide you with her address, in strictest confidence, of course."

"Of course. I shall return with the receipt tomorrow. Thank you for your kind assistance in this matter."

CHAPTER XXVI

Threatening

*P*eter Harries stopped by the local office of the RSPCA, made the agreed to donation and then immediately returned to the Brecon post office, where he again asked to speak with the local Postmaster. He showed him the receipt and in return was handed a slip of paper with a typed address, which said: "Farm house with dark-green door, Near Coed Fenni-fach, Brecon Beacons National Park."

When Harries returned to his bookshop he went back online and googled maps of the Brecon Beacons National Park for an hour before he finally managed to locate Coed Fenni-fach. He immediately drove to the area and soon spotted the only farm cottage with a dark-green front door. Now certain where she lived he returned to Boz Books and sent an e-mail to Yee Kar-Lok, an antiquarian book dealer in Hong Kong.

From:	peter@bozbooks.demon.co.uk
Sent:	Saturday, 14 March 2015 9:26:53
To:	yeekarlokbooks.com.hk
Subject:	CLD Diary

URGENT: Re: Your interest in extreme CLD
rarities. I have located lost 1858 diary. My
client is asking 200,000 pounds sterling. Any
interest please contact at your earliest
convenience. Usual conditions and commission
apply. Complete discretion required.

Five days later two Asian men, wearing blue jeans, black
leather jackets and mirrored sunglasses, entered Boz Books.
They looked around the shop to be sure that there were no
other customers in the shop then one of them turned around
the sign hanging on the front door to indicate that the shop
was closed. They went up to the sales desk where Peter
Harries was seated pricing books for his stock. "Good day,
gentlemen, may I be of some service?"

"Perhaps," the shorter of the two responded. "We would like
to speak to Mr Peter Harries."

"That's me. Who are you?"

"We are on the staff of the Embassy of the Democratic
People's Republic of Korea in London."

"Really? I didn't realize that North Korea has an embassy in the UK."

"Yes, it's on Gunnersbury Avenue."

"I see. How can I be of assistance?"

"We understand that you recently contacted Yee Kar-Lok regarding a certain diary that you are offering for sale. Is this true?"

"Yes, but how did you know that?"

"Mr Yee is Supreme Leader Kim Jong-un's agent for the purchase of certain antiquarian books of interest to him. He has informed us that you can provide this book. Is that correct?"

"Perhaps, though I don't have it here at the shop. The actual owner has possession of the diary. I am her agent for its sale."

"Mr Yee has informed our Embassy that you are asking too high a price for the diary. He is prepared to offer £20,000 sterling."

Harries laughed. "There has been an unfortunate misunderstanding. The asking price for the diary is £200,000 sterling."

"Mr Yee told us that you were asking this absurd price and told us to explain to you that the fair price for the diary is £20,000. That is what we came prepared to give you."

"You don't understand. The diary is not for sale at that price."

"No, Mr Harries, you don't yet seem to understand. This offer is not optional. You will please either produce the diary or tell us where we can pick it up."

Harries stood up. "You need to leave the shop immediately, or I shall be forced to call the police!"

The taller of the two stepped forward and struck Harries hard in the face, breaking his jaw and knocking him unconscious. When he came to he found himself sitting in his chair with his hands tied behind him and bound securely to the chair. He could feel that several of his teeth had been loosened by the blow. "Mr Harries, we are quite serious. Do you have the diary?"

"No," he managed to say.

"Who has it then?"

"I wo'n't tell you," he bravely said, and was instantly struck again by the taller man, this time in his solar plexus. He again passed out, but eventually came to.

"Mr Harries, you will give us the name and address of the person who has the diary or my comrade will slowly and very painfully beat you to death. Do you understand?"

Harries again refused and was struck hard in the face again. He withstood three more horrific, bone shattering blows before agreeing to give them Afanen's name and instructions for how to find her cottage.

Satisfied that they had what they wanted, the taller man struck Harries a final blow that shattered a vertebra in his neck.

CHAPTER **XXVII**

Presenting

*T*he following day Edward Wakeling saw the postman
walking up to his front door and met him to accept the
package. He checked the return address and noticed that it
had been mailed from Brecon. He took the box to the kitchen
where he got out a sharp knife and opened the box and took
out the bundle. After a minute or two he was down to the
final black plastic wrapping and when he pulled it out he
knew instantly what it was. He sat down hard at the kitchen
table and took a minute to catch his breath. He slowly opened
the front cover and saw to his astonishment that it was the
third missing diary.

He went through the packing to see if there was a card or
message, but there was nothing. He knew at once that the
return address was fake. It was as if the diary had come out
of the blue. Glancing out the bay window across the River Wye
towards Wales on the other side he saw a perfect rainbow.

He took the diary into the living room and spent the entire
day reading the diary. So many questioned were answered,
but just as many new one presented themselves as well. By

the end of the day he was emotionally drained and exquisitely happy, all at the same time. He suddenly realized that he was hungry and that he hadn't eaten all day, so he fixed himself a cup of tea and sat awhile in uffish thought trying to imagine who might have sent the diary to him. He finally decided that the only person who might have done it was Afanen. He gave her a ring.

"Hello," Afanen said when she answered.

"Is this Afanen?" he asked.

"Yes. Speaking."

"This is Edward Wakeling."

"Oh, Edward! How nice of you to call. To what do I owe the pleasure?"

"Well, today I received an anonymous gift that was mailed from Brecon. I was wondering if perchance it had come from you?"

"Have you been feeling all right, Edward? You aren't ill are you?"

"No I'm quite fine."

"Now, Edward, you know that I gave you my little Welsh *Alice* when I left your home yesterday evening. Surely you remember!"

"Yes, of course, I remember that quite clearly. This is something else. Did you send me something else?"

She avoided the question. "What is it that you've received, Edward?"

"Can you keep a secret, Afanen?"

"Oh, yes; probably better than anyone you've ever met."

"If I tell you then it must be a very *deep* secret; just between the two of us."

"I promise."

"Someone has sent me the third missing diary. I was wondering if it was from you."

"Now, Edward, I hold our friendship very dear, but I am not so crazy as to send you something worth perhaps several hundred thousand pounds!"

"I suppose that would be quite insane," Edward admitted. "I just ca'n't imagine anyone else who would have sent it to me. I thought it might be you because it was posted in Brecon and we had talked at some length about the missing diaries. If it wasn't you, then I am quite at a loss to guess who it was."

"What will you do with it?" she asked.

"I have no idea. I suppose that eventually I must send it to the Dodgson Estate, since they are the rightful owners, but I ca'n't bear the thought of doing it right away."

"Why would you have to do that immediately? They haven't seen it for at least a hundred years. What would be the big hurry?"

"I see your point. They have absolutely no knowledge that even still exists."

"Exactly! How could they know? I would say that what they don't know ca'n't possibly bother them. You couldn't sell it legally, of course."

"Oh, believe me, Afanen, even if I could I would not. How could I part with such a precious thing?"

"I believe you. My suggestion would be to keep it as long as you enjoy having it and then send it along to the Estate."

There was silence for a few moments. "I agree with you, but I shall not send it to them as long as I am alive. I will leave instructions with my solicitor to return it to them once I have passed on."

"Perfect! You have the joy of possession for as long as you want it and Mr C. L. Dodgson's heirs will some day have a very happy surprise when it is returned."

"Yes, in the end we would all be happy and no one will have been harmed."

"Where will you keep it so that it is safe and secure?"

"I shall have to keep it in a bank vault. It is the only sensible thing. I can visit and see it as often as I wish, even bring it home now and then, but return it."

"That sounds imminently reasonable."

"Thank you, Afanen, for talking with me about this. It's helped me come to a clear decision. Are you sure that you will keep all of this in strictest confidence?"

"I will take your secret with me to my grave."

"Good-by then," he said and rang off.

He went back into the front room and looked through the diary again. Finally he said out loud as if Afanen could hear him, "I know it was you, Afanen. I have no idea how you happened to come by this volume and I am sure that I never shall. But I know it was you and I love you for it."

CHAPTER XXVIII

Resuming

*T*he next day Edward went on-line to *The Times* website to see what else had happened in the world. There were several articles of interest that he noticed:

From *The Times*
Tuesday , 24 March 2015
North Korea returns to Six-party talks after Kim Jong-un receives rare *Alice*
By Anthony Beaverskat
North Korean diplomats have returned to the on-again-off-again Six Party Talks (China, The United States, North and South Korea, and Japan) after Kim Jong-un finally received the copy of the rare first edition (1865) of *Alice's Adventures in Wonderland* that he won on 10 March at Sotheby's (London) for £215,000.

Julia Roberts, Assistant Deputy Under-Secretary of Sate for North Korean Affairs, personally delivered the book to Kim Jong-un after Prime Minister Lynn Truss intervened to ensure that the necessary export licence was approved. Sources in the U.S. Department of State believe that this act of shuttle diplomacy has most likely averted nuclear war on the Korean

Peninsula. The Great Successor, who is a long-time fan of Roberts, was reportedly seen hand-in-hand with the Under-Secretary on the dais at a sumptuous state reception in an indoor stadium where 15,000 school girls wearing *Alice in Wonderland* costumes performed elaborately choreographed dance routines to the music from Walt Disney's version of *Alice In Wonderland* in her honour.

From *The Times*
Tuesday, 24 March 2015
Woman brutally murdered in farmhouse near Welsh town of Coed Fenni-fach
By Cledwyn Prydderch
Mrs Afanen Dyfnallt, a Welsh widow, has been found in her own bed in her picturesque farmhouse inside the boundaries of the Brecon Beacons National Park that is located just across the River Wye. Her throat had been cut and the house ransacked. The motive is assumed to be robbery, but it is unknown what the intruder was looking for or what might have been taken. Brecon Police investigations are continuing. There are no known suspects.

From *The Times*
Tuesday, 24 March 2015
Peter Harries, well-known Hay-on-Wye bookman, found beaten to death
Cledwyn Prydderch
Mr Peter Harries (age unknown), longtime owner of the bookshop Boz Books in the picturesque town of Hay-on-Wye, famous for its many excellent bookshops, has been found beaten to death in his shop. The murder weapon is unknown, but the nature of his injuries suggests that he was probably beaten to death by a martial arts expert. There is speculation that the murder of Mrs Afanen Dyfnallt in her home near Brecon, just across the Welsh border from Hay-on-Wye, may somehow be related. Local Police investigations are continuing. There are no known suspects.

Edward was understandably distressed at the horrific news about his new friend Afanen and also saddened by the death of an old friend, Mr Harries, from whom he had purchased a number of Carrollian books over the years. He immediately rang up the local florist and arranged for a bouquet to be sent to Afanen's home, with instructions to simply leave it outside at the front door if there was no one there to accept it.

Sitting in front of the window that provided a panoramic view of Wales across the River Wye he thought about the momentous events of the past day and couldn't help thinking that the three were somehow related. He was certain that Afanen had given him the missing diary. The fact that she had shown up at Sotheby's for the auction of the 1865 *Alice* made him very suspicious that she might have even been "the Lady" who had sold the book. The first edition of *Alice* also provided a link to Kim Jong-un. Who would have guessed that the Little Monster was an avid Carroll collector, willing to start a nuclear war if the United Kingdom would not allow its export? Could Afanen and Harries have been murdered by someone searching for the missing diary? Would they come looking for him next? It was a frightening possibility, since whoever was looking for it had no scruples about committing murder to get it. Suddenly, a thought passed through his mind. Could it be that Kim Jong-un was the person behind it? Had Harries somehow figured out that Afanen had the diary and approached Kim's Hong Kong buying agent in an attempt to arrange a private, illegal sale? Could Kim have ordered North Korean secret agents to Wales to find it and bring it back to North Korea for his personal Lewis Carroll collection?

The next question he asked himself was whether he had slipped into paranoia.

CHAPTER XXIX

Terrifying

*T*he diminutive Great Successor sat perched atop an expensive red, white and gold silk brocade couch, like a pudgy Caterpillar with buzz-cut hair, sitting atop his magic toadstool, in his personal home-theatre, located (at great human and monetary expense) in a secret, nuclear bomb-proof bunker 1,000 feet beneath his secluded palace at Baekdu-su near the border with China. He was watching, for the thirty-seventh time, Tim Burton's wildly successful gothic retelling of *Alice in Wonderland*. Out of his collection of over 20,000 DVDs, it was number twelve on his all-time list of fifteen top favourite films, after seven starring Elizabeth Taylor, and four starring Julia Roberts. His newly-arrived copy of the 1865 *Alice*, which Julia herself had inscribed for him in violet ink, was resting beside him on his left. Just as Johnny Depp's classic interpretation of the Hatter was dancing across the Mad Tea-party table he was startled by a high-pitched, masculine English voice right beside him on his right. He turned to see, sitting next to him, an apparition of an elderly English vicar. Kim let out a pathetic little high-pitched squeal and sent his fresh-popped bowl of expensive imported "The Kernel" Orville Redenbacher's gourmet popcorn, into which he had mixed a bag of equally expensive plain M&M's, sailing into the garlic-laden air. Leaping from the couch with amazing dexterity for a pudgy little man, the Great Successor began to yell for his guards, but the vicar brought an index finger to his pursed lips and indicated that he should be quiet.

Kim demanded something in Korean.

"If you want me to understand you then you'll need to speak in English."

Kim obliged. "Who are you and how did you get into my private quarters? This area is strictly off-limits!"

"I am the ghost of Charles L. Dodgson and mere physical walls and doors are no hindrance."

"I don't believe in ghosts!"

"You will by the time you leave here."

"What do you want with me?"

"You have something that belongs to me."

"No I don't! Everything in this complex is mine!"

"Not that book," he said, pointing at the *Alice*. "That book is mine."

"You're wrong. I bought that book at Sotheby's. I have the invoice to prove it!"

"It was stolen from my grave. You are therefore in possession of stolen property."'"

"How was I to know that it was stolen? It was offered at public auction. The catalogue didn't specify where it came from or how the owner had obtained it!"

"Your problem, Mr Kim, is that you now have it. And what's more, it's been damaged!"

"It has not!"

"Oh, but it has. Someone has scribbled all over it." The apparition picked up the book, opened it to the half-title and pointed to a bold signature written in purple ink. "I really hate it when people write in my books!"

"That's not damage! That's Julia Roberts' genuine autograph. She inscribed it to me! The book is now more valuable than when I bought it!"

"Who is Julia Roberts?"

Kim was stunned. "Who is Julia Roberts? Where have you been?"

"I've been in my grave until I was recently disturbed, minding my own business. You have no idea how irritating it is to have some dolt disturb you while you're in your grave."

"Well, Julia Roberts is the most beautiful woman that has ever lived. She is an actress and superstar!"

"No, you're wrong! The most beautiful woman who ever lived was a violinist, named Alexandra Kitchin."

"Who was she? I've never heard of her."

"A child-friend I once knew."

"I don't believe anything you're telling me! You're just trying to frighten me! People don't come out of their graves! When they die they just cease to exist and pass into nothingness! You're just an actor. Has the CIA put you up to this stunt?"

"What is the CIA?"

"Are you kidding? The American Central Intelligence Agency!"

"I've never heard of it. I'm not an agent and I'm here in this nightmarish little country of yours on my own."

"Nonsense! Get out of here! Now!"

"You haven't yet apologized."

"Apologized? Apologized for what! I'm Kim Jong-un! I don't offer apologies for anything!"

"You have a very bad attitude, Mr Kim. You must apologize for scribbling in my book. In my realm doing that is a capital offence!"

"Your realm? What or where is *your* realm?"

"The realm of the dead. You really are very slow, Mr Kim."

"I don't believe you!"

"You will, because in just a few more minutes you will inhabit it—permanently!" The apparition suddenly stood up, floating about a foot above the carpet. Kim stumbled backward, trying to get away. Suddenly the apparition's skull appeared, as if the skin, muscles, and eyes had vanished.

Kim Jong-un's blood pressure spiked and unbearable pain radiated down his left arm. Black nausea engulfed him and he hurled half-eaten popcorn and M&M's onto the rare antique Persian carpet before collapsing into his own vomit.

The skeletal apparition casually sat back down and watched the rest of the film. By the time the credits appeared the Great Successor's shade had passed on.

"I may have to pay Mr Burton a visit," the apparition said aloud, though Kim's spirit couldn't hear him, having departed directly for hell. "I'm not very happy with the way he's meddled with my story."

CHAPTER XXX

Concluding

*E*dward turned on his computer to read the news on-line at *The Times* website to see what else had happened. He was almost afraid to look, but happily this time it was very welcome news indeed.

From *The Times*
Thursday, 26 March 2015
**Widespread speculation that North Korea's
Kim Jong-un is dead**
By Lee, Soon-yi
South Korea's *Chosun Ilbo* newspaper reports that The Democratic People's Republic of Korea's (DPRK) Supreme Leader, Kim Jong-un, has suffered a fatal heart attack. Accurate news about anything happening in "The Hermit Kingdom", as it is sometimes referred to, is virtually impossible to obtain, and *The Times* has been unable to verify this report. The ROK's embassy has issued a terse "No comment" statement.

Kim Jong-un, son of the Dear Leader Kim Jong-il and grandson of the Great Leader Kim Il-sung, was born in 1983 or early 1984, making him only 31 or 32 years of age at his alleged death. His rule of North Korea began in December 2011. It has been suggested that his death is likely have been due to a congenital heart condition; his father and grandfather both died from heart attacks.

China's Xinhua news agency reports that both the DPRK and ROK armies are on high alert and China has made an official appeal to all members in the Six-party talks to be calm and wait for developments before making any statements that might exacerbate the already dangerously tense situation.

Julia Roberts, the U.S. government's Assistant Deputy Under-Secretary of State for North Korean Affairs, has issued a statement expressing her "personal profound condolences to the heroic, starving people of The Democratic People's Republic of Korea for the tragic loss of their beloved 'Great Successor' and one of my greatest fans."

"Well," Edward said aloud to himself, "it would appear that at least I needn't worry about being murdered in bed by some North Korean agent!"

Afterword
What Happened to the Diaries?[1]

*C*harles Dodgson kept a personal diary for most of his life. The diary, which he called his private journal, was written up in small notebooks, and by the end of his life, he was writing in volume 13. Since that time, four of these volumes have gone missing, presumed destroyed by someone in the Dodgson family. There has been much speculation about who this might be. Of the surviving nine volumes, ten pages are missing, cut out from the original journal. Was the same family censor at work? What were they trying to hide?

Within the Dodgson Family Archive, now deposited at the Surrey History Centre at Woking, there is an intriguing scrap of paper which is headed "Cut pages in Diary". It has always mystified me why the censor would cut the pages and then keep a record of what was contained on those pages. Such action is illogical. However, I have come to the conclusion that this piece of paper was not written by the censor, but by someone who knew what the censor intended, did not

1 This paper is based on a talk given to the Lewis Carroll Society at the Surrey History Centre, Woking, on Saturday 17 July 2010.

agree with the actions of the censor, and had the opportunity of recording what was about to be lost forever. This makes more sense to me.

Let us go back and describe what happened to the diaries after Dodgson's death. The two executors of Dodgson's estate were his brothers, Wilfred and Edwin. Edwin was far away on the island of St Helena at the time of Dodgson's death in January 1898, in his role as vicar of Jamestown, a post he held from 1896 to 1899. This left all the arrangements to Wilfred. He removed the diaries from Dodgson's rooms at Christ Church, and kept them initially at his current home, The Court, Cleobury North, Shropshire, but later at his address in Ludlow after his retirement in 1902. Almost immediately, his nephew, Stuart Dodgson Collingwood, asked to borrow them because he intended to write a biography of his famous uncle, with the blessing of the Dodgson Family. We know he had access to all 13 volumes of the diary because there are quotes from each volume in his *Life and Letters of Lewis Carroll*, which was published at the end of 1898. The diaries then returned to Wilfred.

According to Roger Lancelyn Green, the first editor of *Lewis Carroll's Diaries* in 1953, and a friend of Dodgson's nieces, he wrote in his "Preface" that at the time of the Centenary celebrations in 1932, the next generation of Dodgson's began to look for their uncle's miscellaneous literary remains, and "the Diaries were found on a cellar floor, having fallen out of a cardboard box: and by then four of the thirteen volumes had disappeared—and no trace of them has since been discovered." This argument lacks credibility. The 13 volumes formed a set, all in similar sized notebooks and bindings, but some fatter than others. If four had fallen out of the cardboard box, surely they couldn't be far away if anyone had taken the opportunity to look for them. There is no evidence that the diaries were divided up at any time. Collingwood had all of them, and gave back all of them.

We have evidence that Wilfred looked after the diaries until his death in December 1914. Some correspondence has come to light which informs us that Wilfred made reference to the diaries and even quoted from various volumes as late as February 1914 (see *Wilfred Dodgson of Shropshire* by David Lansley, White Stone Press, 2011).

Although Edwin Dodgson, now retired and living with his sisters at Guildford, was to live for another four years after Wilfred's death, the role of custodian of the diaries, and executor of the C. L. Dodgson Estate, transferred to Wilfred's eldest son, Charles Hassard Wilfrid Dodgson, known as "Willie" when young, and "Bill" when older, but I will call him CHWD. From 1908, CHWD worked in partnership with his father as Messrs W. L. Dodgson and Son of Ludlow, independent land agents. After the death of his father, CHWD continued running the firm with the help of his younger brother, Reginald. The First World War intervened, and both brothers undertook a role as part of the defence of the country, not strictly military, but affiliated to the territorial army, guarding key installations under threat from the enemy. CHWD became Major to a local Cadet Force. In 1920, he married a war-widow, and moved to Breinton Manor in Herefordshire, a large and imposing country house by the River Wye. The surviving papers of the C. L. Dodgson Estate went with him.

I came across an interesting article published in the *Herefordshire Times* dated 30 January 1932, written by one of their reporters with the pseudonym, "Wyefarer". He had been to Breinton Manor to interview CHWD. He recorded that he discussed the matter of the Lewis Carroll Centenary with CHWD and went on to say that "He exhibited the Lewis Carroll diaries—thirteen closely-written books recording, in clear and open, yet closely-written calligraphy, the author's day-to-day sayings and doings.... Major Dodgson has practically completed the editing of these priceless and fascinating diaries...." If the reporter was right, the 13 volumes of the diaries were still intact at the time of the Lewis Carroll Centenary.

The work of editing the diaries for publication had been suggested because CHWD found the task of responding to numerous enquiries irksome and time-consuming, and he felt that if they were published, albeit in an abridged form, they would serve to answer people's queries directly without the necessity of being involved himself. He enrolled his sister, F. Menella Dodgson, to assist him in this task. They began producing typescripts of the edited version of the diaries that could be published. At the same time, substantial parts of the diary were deemed too personal for the family to divulge, and they were omitted from these typescripts. I should add that some copies of these typescripts survive, but they were never used to publish the diaries. We have emerging among these two Dodgson family members the makings of a censor.

The task of preparing these typescripts began around 1930. CHWD and Menella consulted Falconer Madan, bibliographer of Lewis Carroll's works, and former Librarian of the Bodleian Library, about the Oxford connections mentioned in the diaries. Some interesting correspondence between them survives, now in the Parrish Collection at Princeton University. For example, a letter dated 29 February 1932 from Menella to Madan states: "...we are making a violent effort to finish the typing of all 13 vols. by the end of the week." Assuming this was not a slip of the pen, we have a second piece of evidence that all 13 volumes still existed at the beginning of 1932. CHWD emerges as the "sensitive" one, wishing to hold back information. The following extract from a letter dated 5 July 1931 explains his position: "The editing of the diaries is a formidable job. I have nearly completed the first reading—eliminating anything which is too intimate for publication or of purely family interest." Other letters repeat this stance. In October 1931 he proposed sending Madan some typescripts, but even these were subject to more censorship since CHWD added: "my proposed cuts [are] marked in pencil." He goes on to say "I feel that I may fall between two stools for either I may (as an interested member of the family) retain matter of no interest or I may err on the other side, and leave out matter which, though it might convey nothing to the man in the street, would have some interest or charm to the discriminating reader." In a letter dated 12 November 1931 he indicates: "I have cut, with exceptions here and there, 31 pages out of the 42! and it is not worth having these 31 pages typed." Another letter dated 17 June 1932 discusses Madan's proposal to include the diaries at the Centenary Exhibition in London. CHWD sent volume 4 of the diaries (the year 1856) to Madan for this purpose, but wrote: "I send you one in which the cuts are very mild and suggest (only suggest) page 26 as interesting for exhibition.[2] I understand that the Diary will merely be on show and not handled or read indiscriminately. Will you look through it to find what pages you will like to print. It is only where passages are marked "cut" in the margin that we object to publication. The passages with lines through are merely shortenings." The diary is briefly mentioned in the preliminaries of the Exhibition Catalogue, but in the supplementary list, issued as a separate stitched pamphlet, there is a note to say it was displayed as part of catalogue number 316 (specimens of Dodgson's Photographs). Its role was clearly under-played at the exhibition, probably in an

---

2 About choosing the name "Lewis Carroll".

attempt to draw attention away from this significant piece of literary history, and to appease certain members of the Dodgson Family.

Let us now turn to Frances Menella Dodgson, known as Menella or Nella, who was Wilfred's fourth daughter, and the next child after CHWD. She was party to the plans to edit the diaries and publish them in an abridged form. She worked with CHWD on this project, and the two of them discussed what should be edited out of the published form. Initially this was carried out by letter or occasional visit to Herefordshire, but eventually it became expedient for Menella to move to Breinton Manor for a period of time so that the task could be speeded up. This happened in February 1932 when they hoped to have the diary ready and published sometime in the Centenary year. As far as I am aware, CHWD and Menella used the manuscript diaries to mark the sections to be cut, but a hired typist did the actual work of preparing the typescripts. In some cases, more than one version of the typescripts was made, and copies were produced. These were supplied to the Literary Agent (A. P. Watt) of the Dodgson Family, who tried to secure a publisher, and loaned to people like Madan who were asked to provide background notes. Madan made a trip to see CHWD at Breinton Manor in July 1931, and Menella also made the trip to be there at the same time. This is when Madan saw the actual diaries for the first time—well, he saw nine volumes out of the 13. He did, however, notice that some pages had been removed from the actual diaries, and must have remarked on this fact. Menella wrote to Madan on 11 November 1931: "Let me relieve your mind at once, and say that you will come upon no more missing leaves in the Diary!!!" There is an element of guilt in this statement, but also an underlying tone that such action was to be regretted. I think Menella knew who had removed the pages, but did not condone the action. The censor, it appears to me, was CHWD—he of a sensitive disposition, who felt that some aspects of the diary were for family eyes only, and everybody else should mind their own business. Menella was a different character. She had the instincts of a librarian—fully recognizing the literary legacy that had been entrusted to their care, and realising that serious scholars and researchers would need access to some family documents when working on the life and works of Lewis Carroll. Letters reveal that she kept a detailed record of Dodgson's works in a little red book. She also catalogued references made in the diaries thematically in another notebook. But by working closely with her brother, she was aware of *his* attitude, and may have been horrified to learn that he wished to suppress permanently material in the diaries.

Where does all this lead us? We have two suspects that might have been responsible for the missing volumes of the diaries and some of the missing pages. It is my contention that the censor was Charles Hassard Wilfrid Dodgson (CHWD). He was the custodian of the 13 volumes of the diaries, and it was he who decided, out of expediency, that the diary should be published. But when he came to read through the volumes, he came to the conclusion that there were many references that were about internal family matters, some probably written in a negative way, others of a personal nature, that he felt should not be made public. At this stage, I think he suppressed four of the volumes, probably by destroying them. I think it possible that Menella, who was invited to help him with the task of editing the diaries for publication, knew nothing about the fate of the four missing volumes, and had presumed them lost through neglect. The suggestion that four volumes had become separated from the others, and inadvertently lost, probably came from CHWD as he needed some excuse for them no longer existing.

As the typescripts were being made, various sections of the diaries were discussed between CHWD and Menella, and they exercised an editorial role in omitting various parts of the diary—some sections because they were uninteresting, but others because they were deemed too personal for publication. It is my suggestion that CHWD spoke to Menella about removing some pages so that the content was safely and permanently taken away from any future public gaze. Menella's instincts were that such drastic action with their entrusted literary legacy was a step too far, but in her position, her older brother had the final say. After all, he was the sole Executor of the C. L. Dodgson Estate. On a visit to Breinton Manor, I can imagine that CHWD proposed that certain pages were cut out of the diaries and destroyed. Menella probably found it hopeless to argue against this, but made a mental note of the pages CHWD had in mind. On her return to London, she jotted down the pages that were likely to disappear on a piece of paper that she headed "Cut Pages in Diary." Let me say, at this point, the handwriting of this sheet has been carefully analysed by several people, and the handwriting is undoubtedly that of Menella. I have many examples of letters written by Menella, her sisters, and other members of the Dodgson family. There is no doubt in my mind that Menella wrote out this piece of information, and I think she did it to record an action she did not agree with— the permanent destruction of pages from Dodgson's private journals. In the end, she didn't get it completely right. She mentions three pages, very briefly, that she thinks will be cut—two from Volume 8, and one from volume 11. The first is about Alice Liddell "not improved by being laid up", a matter that was not particularly of concern to the Dodgson family. This page was eventually *not* cut from the diary—the offending sentence has been scrawled over in an attempt to disguise the content. However, a number of us have deciphered the sentence under the scrawl, and it reads: "Alice was in an unusually imperious and ungentle mood by no means improved by being an invalid."

The other two pages mentioned *have* been removed. One concerned the unfounded and potentially damaging gossip that Dodgson hears from Mrs Liddell that he is supposed to be paying too close attention to the Governess, Miss Prickett, and the eldest daughter, Lorina Liddell. The remaining missing page has the brief note that it "is about S.H.D."[3] Underneath these notes is a question that Menella asks that probably refers to the task of editing the diaries that was on her mind. It says: "Does anyone know what the 'business with Lord Newry' was which put L. C.[4] out of 'Mrs Liddell's good graces'."[5]

Clearly, Menella was loyal to her brother, but worried about the pages he intended to cut and destroy, so she recorded, albeit briefly, what information would be suppressed. Two pages disappeared on this occasion, but they were not necessarily the first or the last to be removed from the diaries. There are, in total, 10 missing pages, and I would refer you to my article entitled "What Happened to Lewis Carroll's Diaries" published in *The Carrollian*, No. 8, Autumn 2001, for further details.

At the end of the day, the attempt by CHWD and Menella to publish a very severely edited version of Dodgson's diaries

---

3 That is, concerning Skeffington Hume Dodgson.

4 "Lewis Carroll".

5 Dodgson had voted against a proposal by Lord Newry, then an undergraduate, to hold a Ball at Christ Church, which was against the rules of the college. He had spoken to Newry about the difficulty the college had with the Ball, and had noted that "I am afraid much ill-feeling will result." Mrs Liddell, very friendly with Lord Newry, certainly was not happy with the decision made by senior members of the college.

failed. No publisher would take it, and the project was shelved. When CHWD died in 1941, Menella took over as the sole Executor of the C. L. Dodgson Estate. One of her first tasks was an attempt to list what remained of the Estate spread across the Dodgson Family. Her letters reveal a zeal to conserve and list what remained. She continued to work on the diaries, producing notebooks of information gleaned from its pages, with the help of her sisters. As time went by, she chose her nephew, Philip Dodgson Jaques, to take over the mantle of Executor of the C. L. Dodgson Estate. She died in 1963.

Since then, Menella has been much maligned as the censor and destroyer of the diary pages, which I now think is totally unjustified. Having read scores of her letters over the last decade, she does not come across to me as a person who would do such a thing—it would have been an un-characteristic act. On the other hand, the more I learn about CHWD, the more I am convinced that he was the culprit.

Edward Wakeling

The Oxfordic Oracle

A Tale of Inspector Spectre

BY

BYRON W. SEWELL

AND

AUGUST A. IMHOLTZ, JR

ILLUSTRATED BY

HARRY FURNISS

The Oxfordic Oracle

"To give an accurate and exhaustive account of the peculiar case of the Oxfordic Oracle would need a far less brilliant pen than ours. "

—with apologies to Max Beerbohm

*O*n 2 April 1881 Inspector Ian Spectre of Scotland Yard's clandestine Special Operations Branch (SOB) arrived at the entrance to an ancient house on Holywell Street, an hour before the scheduled midnight meeting of the Oxford Phantasmalogical Society (OPS). There had been numerous reports to Scotland Yard from Oxonians concerning strange goings-on at the OPS: purported Satan worship, séances, blood sacrifices (chickens), and even rituals inspired by Shashan Kali as Chandalini. Strange-looking people, costumed as Druids, modern Wiccans, or ancient Romans, had been seen coming and going late at night. Terrifying, eerie screams had been heard, and worst of all there was a strange odour that continuously emanated from the chimney, sometimes causing the pigeons to swoon and fall from their perches. After dozens of such outrageous reports had accumulated SOB finally had little choice but to send someone undercover to observe exactly what was happening at the OPS. For this assignment, the Superintendent had selected Inspector Ian Spectre, nicknamed "Inspector Inspectre" by his admiring colleagues in the SOB. He was by nature deeply inquisitive and highly sceptical, and even more important for his present assignment, was an accomplished amateur magician.

Inspector Spectre had intentionally arrived early, determined to look around the meeting room before the proceedings had commenced to see if he could find any wires, strings, trap doors, or mirrors that might indicate some planned use of common conjuror's tricks.

Inspector Spectre had taken great pains to establish a credible false identity as one Sir Charles Henry Moxon Skeffingstone of Stranglebleat House, Herts., an imaginary, though plausible-sounding, place. This he had accomplished by the ruse of a lengthy correspondence with a few members of the OPS Board of Governors over the course of several months, expressing his profound interest in metaphysics, phantoms and the fey, and insinuating that he had every intention of investing a portion of his vast wealth in support of psychical research. Needless to say, the OPS Board was very excited by the possibility of a financial windfall, and had determined to make their next meeting, at which Sir Charles would be in attendance, a very memorable event. They had no idea just how memorable it would turn out to be.

The house was completely dark and shuttered, and Inspector Spectre had to strike a match for enough light to read the brass numerals 42 on the door to be certain that he had found the correct address. Holywell Street itself was almost as dark as the house, there being no moon as yet and the only functioning street lamp at least fifty yards distant. Certain that he had found the correct house, Inspector Spectre struck the brass knocker boldly three times and waited.

A few minutes later he heard a muffled voice through the door. "Who is it? What do you want?"

"Charles Skeffingstone!" he bellowed, so as to be heard through the thick door.

The door almost instantly opened, revealing a beautiful young woman dressed provocatively in a very revealing white diaphanous robe and holding a candle level with her face. "You're early," she said. "The meeting starts at midnight."

"Madame, if I leave I shall not return."

She instantly stepped back. "Come in; come in," she said. "Do come in! We will be holding the meeting in the library. You can wait there until the others have arrived. Please follow me, Sir Skeffinton."

"My name is Skeffingstone," he corrected her as he followed. "Skeffing-*stone*."

"Begging your pardon, I'm sure," she said over her shoulder. "It's an unfamiliar name to me."

"And what might your name be, Miss?"

"My name is Cassandra Pythia."

"Ah! A prophetess's name! Surely not your own, however."

She turned and faced the Inspector. "I am an actress, Sir, and that is my stage name."

"I see. What's your real name then?"

"Karoline, if you really must know, but I wo'n't tell you my family name. That's a secret I shall take to my grave. I have disowned them!"

"That's very dramatic!" he said. "I dare say that there is a fascinating story behind that statement. I notice that you're not an Oxonian, Miss Pythia."

"What makes you think that?"

"I detect a faint Scouse accent."

"Really?" Her face suddenly clouded over and she shook her head in despair.

"What's wrong?"

"I've toiled for ten years to rid myself of that wretched accent, and yet you pick up on it with ease."

"Why would you want to be rid of it?"

"I'm convinced that no one with a Liverpool accent will ever have any more of a chance at a successful stage career than a beetle would have of becoming an accomplished musician!"

"I dare say you're right. I shouldn't have mentioned it. I'm sorry. Actually, you've almost managed to erase it," he assured her. "It's ever so faint, and I know that it's no easy task to lose it. I spent a good part of my childhood in Liverpool, and I am also a Scouse speaker."

"I see. That would explain why you are able to identify it so precisely, I suppose," she said, turning back to lead him down the long hallway.

The library was large and well appointed, with floor-to-ceiling dark oak bookcases around the walls, though perhaps only half of the shelves were full of books. There was a large table with a brass candelabrum having six lit candles set in the middle, and several dozen chairs arranged about the room on threadbare carpets, along with a very peculiar tripod-shaped object with an obvious pipe running up through the floor in front of it. Cassandra lit three individual candles that were sitting on the mantelpiece.

"What is that faint, peculiar odour that lingers everywhere?" he asked.

"It's from natural gases that seep up from between the stones in the cellar floor."

"Is the house built on top of a cemetery?"

"The house is at least four-hundred years old, so I wouldn't have any way of knowing. But you will notice that the odour is not putrid, like one sometimes smells in a crowded church graveyard, so it's not the gases from decomposing corpses, if that was your meaning."

"What sort of gases, then?"

"I'm not a chemist. However, Herr Kolbe, says that he believes that the gases are largely methane and elayl."

"Elayl? What is that?"

"I'm sure I don't know. Perhaps you can ask him. I believe that he plans to attend tonight's meeting."

"You said 'Herr Kolbe'. What is his full name?"

She shrugged. "His first name is Adolf."

"Would that be Lyon Playfair's German assistant, by any chance?"

"I really don't know all of these things you seem so curious about! I'm just an actress!"

"Is that why you are dressed as a Greek goddess? Are we to enjoy a tableau during tonight's meeting?"

"I am not dressed as a goddess. I am costumed as a Delphic virginal priestess. I will attempt to foretell the future tonight, if the prophetic gases cooperate."

"By 'the gases' I assume you mean the elayl?"

"Yes. Elayl often has this affect upon me."

"Have any of your prophetic utterances been fulfilled?"

"I'm told that some of them have. However, when I come out of the trance I have no memory of what I have uttered and I must rely on someone else to tell me the prophecy. But even when I have heard it I never understand a thing of it. I'm just a medium. You'll have to excuse me, Sir Charles; I have things to do to get ready for the meeting."

"Before you go, what is that peculiar tripod stool over there?" He pointed at it.

"That is the Oracle's Throne. I sit upon it when I attempt to peer into the future or commune with departed spirits."

"And what is the purpose of the pipe protruding through the floor?"

"That comes up from the cellar. The gases that accumulate there flow up the pipe and emerge in front of the Throne. I sit there, breathing the mysterious vapours, and wait for their affects to give rise to a prophecy."

Inspector Spectre walked over to the pipe. "It's got a cork in it."

"Of course it does. Otherwise the gases might fill the library. They can be explosive if allowed to accumulate. A candle can easily ignite them. I will uncork the pipe when it is time to prophesy."

"Why doesn't the cellar fill up with these gases and explode?"

"It would, except for the fireplace."

"Fireplace? You have a fireplace in the cellar with flammable vapours? What madness is that?"

"Oh, it's never lit! We aren't fools! The chimney serves as a means for the gases to safely exit the house—the natural draft of the chimney pulls them out and discharges them harmlessly to the atmosphere. When we wish to hear from the Oracle we close the damper slightly, and the gases begin to rise up the pipe."

"Why don't you simply go to the cellar to hear from the Oracle? I believe that in Delphi the virginal priestesses went down into an underground cave."

"It's dark down there and too dangerous to take a candle or lantern. By doing it this way we have a means for regulating the flow and to keep from blowing up the house."

"I see; very interesting and clever!"

"I really must excuse myself this very moment!"

"Yes, yes; of course. Sorry to have delayed you."

"Do make yourself comfortable, Sir Steppingstone."

"*Skeffing*-stone," he corrected her.

"Yes, of course! Sorry! I may never get it right!"

When she had left, Inspector Spectre went over to one of the bookcases, curious about what sort of library he would find in this strange house. He pulled a book down at random and took it over near a candle to better see it. The cover felt damp. When he opened the book he saw that the text was in German and that the leaves were spotted with large greenish-gray splotches. He lifted it to his nose and smelled it carefully, taking tiny breaths, so as not to inhale clouds of spores. It had a pungent mildew odour. He jerked it away from his face in disgust and tossed it onto the hearth. The book was so damp that it didn't instantly ignite, but rather lay on the grate, smoldering and steaming.

He took one of the candlesticks down from the mantelpiece and carried it over to examine the bookcases, discovering that almost every book, and even the cases themselves, had been attacked to some degree by the insidious greyish-green mould.

He returned to the middle of the room and examined the table, searching for camouflaged wires, or evidence of hidden compartments, but found nothing. If there were such things built into the table then they had been very cleverly concealed.

As Inspector Spectre was examining the table he heard a loud knock at the door. He looked up just in time to see Cassandra hurry past the library door, her Greek costume making her look eerily like a phantom floating past. He heard her open the heavy front door and then greet the new arrivals. "Mr Schiller, how nice to see you!"

"Good evening, Cassie!" a man answered. "Cassie, this is the Reverend Charles Dodgson, reader in mathematics at Christ Church. Mr Dodgson, this is Cassandra Pythia."

"Is it possible that this is your real name?" Dodgson asked in a kindly tone.

"No, Mr Dodgson. I am an actress and that is my stage name. I never use my original name, which I detest."

"I see. It's pleasant to meet you, Mrs Pythia."

"It's Miss Pythia. I'm not married."

"Nor I," Dodgson said, unable to keep from flirting with a beautiful young woman.

"Come into the library, wo'n't you?" Cassandra said. "We already have one guest."

In a few moments Cassandra entered the library with the two men in tow. Inspector Spectre did not recognize either of them.

"Sir Charles Schleppingfoam, I'd like for you to meet Mr Fernando Caning Scott Schiller." Dodgson held back.

Inspector Spectre extended his hand. "Actually, my name is Charles Skeffingstone," he said. "How do you do?"

"Very well, thank you. And actually, my first name is Ferdinand."

They laughed.

"Oh dear! I am sorry!" Cassandra said. "I am having a great deal of trouble with names tonight!"

"That's quite all right, Cassie. Never you mind!" He then turned back to Inspector Spectre.

"How long have you been undercover, Constable?" he asked.

This caught Inspector Spectre quite off guard, and he covered this by laughing loudly. "I'm afraid you have confused me with someone else, Sir. I am a country squire. Farming is my life. Cattle. Sheep. A few prize hogs."

Schiller was sceptical; in his opinion Sir Charles had the bearing and mannerisms of a policeman, but he decided to let it drop.

"Mr Dodd," Cassandra continued, "may I present Sir Charles Skeffington? Sir Charles, this is the Reverend Charles Dodd, mathematics lecturer at Christ Church."

Inspector Spectre extended his hand, which Dodgson took and shook stiffly. "Good evening, Mr Schiller. Actually, my last name is Dodgson."

Cassandra laughed a nervously. "Sorry!"

"It's quite all right," Dodgson assured her.

"Mr Schiller has just moved to Oxford. He will be studying philosophy at Balliol. Isn't that exciting?"

"A serious waste of time," Dodgson said bluntly. "All one needs to do is read the Bible to discover Truth."

"Spoken like a cleric," Schiller remarked, not the least intimidated by Dodgson's remarks. "Most ministers that I have ever met have closed minds to anything other than traditional religion. Is your mind closed, Mr Dodgson?"

"If it was then I wouldn't be here tonight. I believe in other planes of reality and existence."

"Really? That's quite amazing! By that do you mean that you believe in ghosts?" He grinned.

"Of course," Dodgson replied matter-of-factly.

"And fairies?" Schiller asked, surprised again by Dodgson admission.

"Absolutely!"

"Absolutely?"

"Quite."

"Tell me, Mr Dodgson, have you ever actually seen a fairy?" Schiller asked, quite confident that he would have to admit that he hadn't.

"Not in the natural plane, though I do believe that they do sometimes materialize here; but I have seen them often in the interface between the natural and ethereal planes."

"Do you mean in your dreams?"

"No, I mean the state between being awake and on the verge of sleep; what I refer to as the 'eerie' state. We often pass through this state so quickly that we don't realize its existence, going deeper into sleep and dreams. But if one learns to suspend oneself in this eerie state he will often encounter fairies and elves. I have never seen ghosts there, however, though they may well inhabit that realm as well."

"How many times have you experienced this?" Schiller asked, still sceptical, but fascinated by Dodgson's strange ideas, spoken with such quiet conviction.

"I don't keep records of them. But it has happened many times. Many."

"How about you, Sir Charles?" Schiller asked, turning to Inspector Spectre. "Do you believe in fairies, too?"

"I ca'n't say that I do or that I don't. I have never seen them, so I ca'n't speak about them from a personal perspective. But I have a great interest in metaphysics. I have decided to invest some significant sums in psychical research. My interest lies in contacting departed spirits."

"Why?" Schiller asked. "Do you want to contact a dead mother or perhaps a wife?"

"My mother is still alive and I have never married, nor do I plan to. I would simply like to have discourse with entities that have long departed this present age. I have many unanswered questions about the afterlife."

"Such as?" Schiller asked.

"Oh, fundamental things, such as the reality of Heaven and Hell."

"The Bible is quite explicit about the reality of Heaven," Dodgson interjected. "You needn't waste your personal fortune trying to find out about that! Heaven is certainly a reality."

"And Hell, as well," interjected Cassandra, trying to join in on the conversation.

"No, the Bible does not actually support that view," Dodgson said. "That concept is based upon a misinterpretation of the original Greek text. There is no place of eternal punishment for men and women. Such a concept is inconsistent and incompatible with the very nature of a loving God."

"I agree that there is no Hell," Schiller said, "though not for the same reasons. I don't believe there is a Heaven, or even a God for that matter. There is just Nature, which is constantly evolving in response to our thought or conceptions of it."

"So, then," Dodgson said, "you are an atheist. Sadly, Oxford is beginning to fill up with them!"

"I don't claim the atheist label, though it might well apply. I regard myself as a Pragmatist."

Their small polemic was interrupted by yet another knock at the front door.

"Excuse me, Gentlemen," Cassandra said, "l need to answer the door. Please make yourselves comfortable, and do try not to come to blows over any philosophical differences!" She turned and floated off to the front door. "Ah! Herr Kolbe!" Cassandra said when she opened the door. "How nice to see you again!"

"*Guten Abend!*" he responded, taking her hand and kissing it passionately. "*Wie geht es Ihnen?*"

"*Gut, danke, und Ihnen?*"

"*Auch gut, danke!*"

"Now, that is the extent of my German, Herr Kolbe! You must switch to English if we are to converse any further!"

"All right. Dat vill not the problems be any!" he assured her. "I see dat you are wearink the Delphic Oracle dressing gown dis evenink! So, we shall hear the prophecies, no? Yes?"

"Yes, if the gases cooperate!" Cassandra replied, then giggled.

"Oh, dey vill! Dey vill! I declare hit!"

"Good! Come into the library. We have several people here already."

They soon entered the library, where the others were standing in a rough semi-circle awaiting their arrival. Herr Kolbe was dressed formally, having come directly from a dinner party. In sharp contrast, Dodgson was wearing a dressing gown. Schiller was wearing a long dark jacket and tie, and Inspector Spectre was costumed in tweeds for his undercover role.

Cassandra made the introductions, butchering their names.

Herr Kolbe took a deep, audible breath, smelling the air like a hyena trying to catch the scent of a kill on the air. "Ah!" he said loudly. "The sweet smell of elayl! We should have an entertaining evenink, I'm thinkink!"

"I'm glad that you mentioned elayl," Inspector Spectre said to Herr Kolbe. "Earlier this evening I was having a discussion with Miss Pythia. Exactly what is 'elayl'?"

"You may be knowing hit by another name. A few years ago many chemists began calling hit by a new name—ethene."

"No, I've never heard of that name either. Where does this gas come from? I must admit that I know very little about chemistry."

"Elayl is a by-product of the decompostionink of the vegetable matters. Hit is everywhere in nature, though not so often is it so concentrated as in dis *Haus*!"

"Decomposition of vegetable matter? Do you mean the gases given off from rotting rubbish?"

"*Ja!* Sometink like dat! Also comes *mit* hit the methane."

"Why is it in the cellar? Do they just toss their rubbish there?"

"No, of course not! This is from the ancient rubbishes. One can only guesses make! Dis *Haus* is very old! I'm thinkink dat the ancients builded hit on top of a tip. Maybe there vas a deep cave or a well *und* dey just dumped the rubbishes there inside. When hit got full dey covered the stinkink opening *mit den* soils *und* rocks. Over time dey forgotted dat hit vas dere *und* dey builded dis *Haus* on top of die tipple. The gases half been comink up through the cellar since ever."

"Are the gases dangerous?" Dodgson asked, suddenly a bit nervous at being in the house.

"*Ja*, dey can be. Too much of the gases *und* KABOOM! If you bring in a candle or light up the pipe. Too much gases *und* not enough of the air *und* you canst *ersticken*. *Was ist* the *ersticken* in English? I ca'n't remember!"

"Suffocate," Schiller told him.

"*Ja!* Dat's hit! The suffocate. Maybe you even die."

"Perhaps we should open some windows," Dodgson suggested.

"*Nein! Nein!* We wish for *die* Oracle to speak, no? She must enjoy the gases! Hit's a risk. Maybe we hear the interestink prophecies. Maybe we get blow to the bits! Either way hit will be the interestink experience, *nicht?*"

"Yes," Dodgson agreed. "Either way."

"At least we will be able to settle the Heaven-Hell question amongst ourselves, once and for all if we get blown into eternity," Schiller said, grinning.

"*Was ist* the Heaven-Hell question?" Herr Kolbe asked.

"Mr Dodgson and I were having a dispute about the reality of Heaven and Hell before you arrived. He maintains that Heaven exists, but that Hell doesn't. My position is that neither do."

"Oh, I am quite sure dey both do!" Herr Kolbe assured him. "Heaven is a lovely piece of the salmon for dinner. Hell is no white wine to wash hit down *mit!*" He laughed loudly at his small, blasphemous joke and Schiller joined him. Dodgson scowled, afraid that lightning might strike, sure that if it did the ethene-filled house would go up with a bang.

There was another knock at the door and once again Cassandra floated away phantomwise to answer the door. Soon the other guests heard her. "Ah! Mrs Wilcox! Do come in!"

Hearing the family name Dodgson suddenly panicked, afraid that if might be one of his cousins. He quickly moved to a dark corner.

A few moments later Cassandra came into the library, arm-in-arm with a very heavyset middle-aged woman that Dodgson didn't recognize. Greatly relieved, he came out of the shadows and rejoined the group.

"Gentlemen, may I introduce Mrs Edith Wilcox? Mrs Wilcox, this is Mr Fernando Schiller, a student of philosophy at Balliol. This is Sir Charles Steppingstone, who farms in Strangemeat House in Herts. This is the Reverend Charles Dodd, who lectures on mathematics at Christ Church. And this is Herr Adolphe Kolbe, the famous chemist!"

No one bothered to correct their names, all resigned to being called whatever Cassandra came up with on the spur of the moment. Everyone except Herr Kolbe tipped their heads to acknowledge Mrs Wilcox. Herr Kolbe took her hand and kissed it passionately, then clicked his heels together. Edith Wilcox almost swooned.

"Good evening, Gentlemen," Mrs Wilcox said when she had recovered her composure. "It's very nice to meet all of you. I've been very anxious to attend tonight's meeting. This is my first time."

"Do you believe in ghosts, Mrs Wilcox?" Schiller asked.

"I don't know," she said. "I've never seen nor heard one. But I like to think that they might exist—as long as they're friendly—and well fed!"

Everyone except Dodgson laughed at her little joke.

"Mr Dodgson claims to have encountered phantoms on many occasions—as well as fairies and even elves," Schiller said, looking at Dodgson as he spoke, and grinning.

"How wonderful!" Mrs Wilcox gushed. "I do hope that we will see at least one tonight! Do you think we might, Mr Dodgson?"

"I doubt it, Madame, as there is considerable disbelief in their existence amongst us."

"He means me," Schiller said, then smiled at Dodgson.

"Why don't you believe in them, Mr Schiller?" she asked.

"I don't believe in them simply because I've never experienced them."

"Tonight just might be your lucky night, old boy!" Inspector Spectre interjected.

"We'll see," Schiller replied. "Mr Dodgson also believes in Heaven, but not Hell," he added, speaking to Mrs Wilcox.

"How quaint!" Mrs Wilcox observed. "It sounds a bit like wishful thinking, I must say, Mr Dodgson."

Schiller snickered.

"It is not wishful thinking, Madame! It is a simple matter of correctly translating the New Testament Greek text. I'm writing a pamphlet about it. I would be most happy to send you a complimentary copy when it is published if you will provide me with your address."

"Oh, indeed!" She immediately dug into her large handbag and produced a bent calling card, which she handed to Dodgson. "I would be very interested in reading your hellish analysis. I do so hope that you're right about that point! I must admit that I have always been a bit nervous about the possibility of spending eternity in the cellar, as it were."

"Rest assured, Mrs Wilcox, that there is simply no such possibility. By the way, you might be interested to know that Mr Schiller is a self-proclaimed Pragmatist."

"A pragmatist?" Mrs Wilcox asked. "Are you Greek?"

"What I mean by that, Mrs Wilcox, is that Mr Schiller is an atheist," Dodgson explained. "He neither believes in nor trusts in God. Rather, he looks to his own intellect—his mind!—for finding the Truth. Is that correct, Mr Schiller."

"Not precisely, though I do admit that I have no belief in the God of the Bible. I believe in the Man-God, that we live our life perceiving the world through our intellect and thoughts, and that when we die we die. There is nothing more."

"Nothing?" Mrs Wilcox asked.

"Nothing, Madame. Absolutely nothing!"

"Then what is the purpose of our existence?" she asked.

"We exist to think, for by doing so we cause the Universe to evolve into something better, more advanced."

"We exist to think?" Mrs Wilcox asked, surprised to find this out at last.

"Yes, Madame. Thought—the mind—is the ultimate reality. Thought allows us to search for Truth."

"The truth is, Mr Schiller," Mrs Wilcox said, "is that I'm not a very good thinker!"

Everyone laughed, even Schiller.

"A pity, Mrs Wilcox. If you were a good thinker then the world would become a better place for your having been born."

"Yes, well, there you are! Some of us are very clever at thinking and discovering things—like the Truth or a good recipe for pudding. Others of us are quite content to let someone else do the heavy thinking for us. How about you, Herr Kolbe? Are you a heavy thinker?"

"Indeed, Madame. I do a great deal of the heavy thinkink."

"Marvelous! What do you think about?"

"Chemistry. I think most about the chemistry. I wish to understand the structure of the matters. How chemicals are formed. How to join little chemicals to make the bigger chemicals. It is a most fascinating subject to think about!"

"I'm sure it must be!" Mrs Wilcox agreed. "Tell me, Herr Kolbe, what do you think about the possibility of talking to the dead?"

Her strange question caught him off guard. "This has nothink to do with the chemistry, Madame!"

"Oh, I know! It's just something that I am personally interested in. What little thinking I indulge in I do to see if I can find out some way to converse with my dear, departed husband, Nicholas. I would very much like to speak to Nick, if only ever so briefly!"

"You might not like what he has to say," Inspector Spectre suggested.

"What do you mean?" she asked. "I just want to ask him if he's alright. If he can see me. Just find a little comfort."

"What Sir Charles means," Schiller said, "is that your dear departed Nicholas might be in Torment. You might wish you had never heard him. It might be better to live in blissful ignorance, thinking that he is in Mr Dodgson's happy, Heavenly realm with the angels."

"What do you mean by 'in torment'? We laid him to rest in his peaceful grave. We are members of the Church of England and attend services at least twice a year! He was christened there as an infant. We were married in a church! Why wouldn't he be at peace in Heaven?"

"Of course he is at peace, Mrs Wilcox," Dodgson assured her. "God, in His infinite love, would not allow your husband to be anywhere else but in Heaven!"

A sudden expression of relief flooded over her face. "Of course not!" she agreed. "The very thought of my dear Nick being anywhere else but in Heaven would be too much to bear!"

"Exactly!" Dodgson agreed.

"Even if he wasn't perfect!" she added.

"None of us are!" Dodgson agreed. "God is faithful to forgive us our sins if we confess them."

Mrs Wilcox looked worried again. "Nick wasn't one to do a great deal of praying—or confessing."

"Perhaps you will be fortunate enough to hear from your dear departed tonight," Dodgson said, ignoring her implication.

Over the next fifteen minutes several dozen members of the OPS arrived, filling all of the available seating except the President's chair. Most of them would have to stand through the proceedings. The current President of the OPS, Sir

T. Roger Lodyte, finally came into the room and made his way over to where Dodgson, Schiller, Kolbe and Mrs Wilcox were standing. Herr Kolbe introduced him to newcomers Dodgson and Wilcox.

Once Lodyte had met all of the first time visitors he made his way to the President's chair and said, in a very loud voice, "Shall we begin the meeting?"

At this signal Cassandra went directly to the Tripod of Prophesy, uncorked the pipe leading to the cellar, and then seated herself on the strange stool, her face directly over the open end of the pipe. Everyone waited patiently, while Cassandra commenced to take very deep breaths.

"Are we supposed to do anything?" Dodgson asked Herr Kolbe, who was standing next to him.

"Like what?" Kolbe asked.

Dodgson shrugged. "I'm not sure. Chant something, perhaps?"

"Chant what?" Kolbe asked.

"I don't know," Dodgson admitted. "A Sanskrit mantra, perhaps."

"*Nein.* We just wait. Either the mysterious gases will do their work or they wo'n't."

"What should we expect if they happen to work?" Dodgson asked.

"Sometimes Cassie speaks to departed souls. It can be very interesting at times, but you never can tell. At the last meeting she spoke with the spirit of a French peasant who told us that he had died of starvation in 1358."

"Really?" Dodgson said. "How fascinating!"

"Not really. All he wanted to talk about was potatoes *und* his achink back! It was quite borink, really!"

"I was rather hoping that she might converse with someone like the Queen of Sheba or William Shakespeare."

"On can always hope springs eternal! But most of the time she gets in contact with someone who knows nothink of interest! Nothink!"

"Well, I suppose that makes sense," Dodgson admitted.

"Only one person in a million would be a famous historical figure."

"Exactly!" Herr Kolbe agreed. "Terrible odds! Needle in the hayrick. Grain of sand on the seashore. Minnow in the ocean..."

"I understand!" Dodgson said, stopping him. "You're absolutely right!"

They continued to wait on the prophetic gases as Cassandra took ever longer and deeper breaths. Then quite suddenly she spoke. "Get that sheet there on the table and bring it over to me!"

The person closest to it took it to her. Cassandra draped it over her head, letting it hang down over the end of the pipe.

"What's she doing?" Dodgson asked Herr Kolbe.

"There must not be so many of the gases tonight. I'm guessing that she is trying to trap them in the funnel made by the sheet, so dat dey go up to her noses."

"That makes sense!" Dodgson said. "It might help."

They waited for another five minutes while Cassandra huffed and puffed under the sheet like a steam engine. Quite unexpectedly she suddenly tossed off the sheet and looked at the mantelpiece.

"Here is comink the first prophecy!" Herr Kolbe said to Dodgson, his voice revealing great excitement and anticipation.

"There's a buffalo on the chimney-piece!" she screamed, pointing at the mantelpiece, her face registering terror.

Everyone looked where she was pointing, but saw nothing except two cracked Staffordshire dogs, three candlesticks and a dark painting of Whitby, the abbey ruins high on the cliff overlooking a storm-tossed North Sea; definitely no buffalo, though—not even a small ceramic figurine.

"No! Wait a minute! That's not a buffalo!" Cassandra screamed. "That's my sister Becky's husband's niece, Elizabeth! What are you doing up there, Lizzie?" she demanded. "Get down from there right now, or I shall call the Police!"

"Has she lost her mind?" Dodgson asked Herr Kolbe.

"*Nein! Nein!* Hit's the gases. She is havink the hallucinations!"

"I thought she was supposed to foretell the future or give advice!" Dodgson said.

"Sometimes the Oracle speaks the prophecy. Sometimes what she says is very frightening. Some of the times—like this time—it's quite silly and very funny! You never know with the gases!" He laughed softly. "*Das ist gut*," he said, "*nicht?*"

"Look out!" Cassandra suddenly screamed, then held her hands up over her head, as if something was swooping or diving at her. "How did that big bird get in here?" she demanded. "Look out! It's an albatross! Watch it! He'll hit the lamp!"

Everyone looked over at the candelabrum in the middle of the large table where Cassandra was pointing.

"No! Wait a minute! I'm sorry! That's just a postage stamp!" Then she prophesied that "Someday the Post will be delivered through the air by birds!" This prophecy caused a great deal of laughter amongst the crowd. "Someone get that stamp out of here!" she demanded. "It's too damp in here. It'll stick to something and be ruined!"

"She's right about that!" Inspector Spectre agreed, speaking to Dodgson. "It is too damp in here! All of the books that you see are mildewed. Total loss! Smell like the devil, too!"

Several more minutes passed before the Oracle spoke again. "I see three badgers," she said. "They're fighting amongst themselves for control of a mound of dirt!"

"Dis could be a prophecy," Herr Kolbe told Dodgson.

"A prophecy about badgers?"

"*Ja.* Sometimes the Oracle speaks in the riddles. The three badgers could represent three kings who will go to war over control of some contested lands."

"Oh," Dodgson said.

"I hear singing!" the Oracle said. "It sounds like someone is singing underwater. There! Over there!" she screamed, pointing towards the library door. "I see them now. Three beautiful herrings! They are singing!"

"Singing fish?" Dodgson said to Herr Kolbe. "What might they represent? Three queens?"

"*Ja*, could be. Three queens whose realms are islands, surrounded by the seas."

Dodgson tried to think who these queens might be. "Queen Victoria could be one of them," he suggested to Herr Kolbe. "England is an island, after all."

"*Ja!* Could be!"

"Who else?" Dodgson asked.

"I know not," Herr Kolbe admitted. "Name some islands."

Dodgson thought for a moment. "Crete. Cyprus. The Canaries. Malta. Ceylon. Iceland—"

"Are any of them havink the queen?"

"I don't know. The ones that are British colonies do, but that would be double counting. I don't think so."

"Maybe two of them will someday in the distant future be. Cassie might be seeing into the future."

"They bleat! They bleat!" Cassandra declared, tears coming to her eyes.

"Who does?" Dodgson asked Herr Kolbe. "The badgers or the fish?"

"I don't think the badgers bleat," Herr Kolbe said. "I'm thinkink dey growl. It must be the fishes."

"I don't know if herrings bleat," Dodgson said. "Perhaps they do. Some fishes make noises."

Suddenly Cassandra screamed, "You shall have buns! If you'll behave! Yes, buns! Lots of buns!"

"Who will?" Dodgson asked Herr Kolbe.

Herr Kolbe shrugged. "I don't know. "Do badgers eat buns? Do fish?"

"It seems unlikely," Dodgson said. "Birds do, I believe."

"What birds?"

"Perhaps the albatross eats them," Dodgson suggested. "Do albatross eat buns?"

"Who can know such things?" asked Herr Kolbe. "I have never been seeink the albatrosses. But where would an albatross find a bun? I'm not thinkink that it's so easy to find a bun in the middle of the Pacific Ocean. Dey would get all the soggy mess!"

"True," Dodgson agreed. "Unless sailors toss them to them, I suppose."

"Maybe the bun represents agricultural production," suggested Herr Kolbe. "If the three warring kings will quit fighting, then their peoples will have enough food to eat. If they don't behave den comes the famine and dey are all starvink to the death!"

Dodgson found the entire thing quite hopeless, and gave up trying to interpret the prophecy, if that's what it truly was. "I don't know," he said. "I think that it's a rather poor sort of prophecy, but it might make a lovely nonsense poem."

"Perhaps you are being the correct," Herr Kolbe said. "Sometimes the gases just make the Oracle speak the utter nonsense! But it can be quite amusing, *nicht?*"

Cassandra suddenly sat bolt upright and stared briefly, then her eyes rolled up into their sockets and she passed into a deep trance. Without introduction she suddenly began to speak in a man's voice, in fluent German:

"Die Vernunft ist Geist, indem die Gewißheit, alle Realität zu sein, zur Wahrheit erhoben, und sie sich ihrer selbst als ihrer Welt und der Welt als ihrer selbst bewußt ist.—Das Werden des Geistes zeigte die unmittelbar vorhergehende Bewegung auf worin der Gegenstand des Bewußtseins, die reine Kategorie, zum Begriffe der Vernunft sich erhob. In der beobachtenden Vernunft ist diese reine Einheit des Ich und des Seins, des Für-sich- und des An-sich-seins, als das An- sich oder als Sein bestimmt, und das Bewußtsein der Vernunft findet sie. Aber die Wahrheit des Beobachtens ist vielmehr das Aufheben dieses unmittelbaren findenden Instinkts, dieses bewußtlosen Daseins derselben. Die ange- schaute Kategorie, das gefundne Ding tritt in das Bewußtsein als das Für-sich-sein des Ich, welches sich nun im gegenständlichen Wesen als das Selbst weißt. Aber diese Bestimmung der Kategorie, als des Für-sich-seins ent- gegengesetzt dem An-sich-sein, ist ebenso einseitig und ein sich selbst aufhebendes Moment. Die Kategorie wird daher für das Bewußtsein bestimmt, wie sie in ihrer allgemeinen Wahrheit ist als an- und fürsichseiendes Wesen. Diese noch abstrakte Bestimmung, welche die Sache selbst ausmacht, ist erst das geistige Wesen, und sein Bewußtsein ein formales Wissen von ihm, das sich mit mancherlei Inhalt desselben herumtreibt; es ist von der Substanz in der Tat noch als ein

Einzelnes unterschieden, gibt entweder willkürliche Gesetze, oder meint die Gesetze, wie sie an und für sich sind, in seinem Wissen als solchem zu haben; und halt sich für die beurteilende Macht derselben.—Oder von der Seite der Substanz betrachtet, so ist diese das an- und fürsichseiende geistige Wesen, welches noch nicht Bewußtsein seiner selbst ist.—Das an- und fürsichseiende Wesen aber, welches sich zugleich als Bewußtsein wirklich und sich sich selbst vorstellt, ist der Geist."

"Mein Gott!" declared Herr Kolbe. "Listen to her! She's speaking in absolutely fluent German! No accent! Perfect! How is dis possible? She knows no German. Believe me! I ca'n't even speak German dat well!"

"She's an actress," Dodgson suggested. "Perhaps she has memorized it."

"But it is flawless! How can one speak the perfect German by memorizing hit out of a book? No, hit's not the possibility! You must speak the German from your soul to speak hit *mit* such beauty! Such precision!"

"What is she saying?" Dodgson asked. "I know a little German, but she speaks too swiftly and uses so many words that I do not know."

"I recognize it," interjected Schiller. "She's quoting that idiot, Hegel."

"Hegel? Georg Wilhelm Friedrich Hegel?"

"Yes, it's from his book *Phänomenologie des Geistes*, which was published in 1807."

"How do you know this?" Dodgson asked.

"I've been reading him at Balliol as part of my studies," Schiller explained. "Such absolute muddle-headed tripe!"

"But tripe spoken beautifully!" insisted Herr Kolbe.

"Perhaps Cassandra isn't who she claims to be," suggested Inspector Spectre, who had been listening intently to their conversation.

"What do you mean?" Schiller asked, turning to him.

"She could be a German, pretending to be an English actress from Liverpool. She admitted to me earlier that her real name is not Cassandra Pythia. She could be almost anyone."

"I hope that she's not planning on reciting the entire text!" Schiller said, ignoring Inspector Spectre's bizarre ideas.

"This is certainly more interestink than listening to some dead Frenchman potato farmer!" Herr Kolbe insisted.

"Barely!" responded Schiller, who obviously had a very low opinion of Hegel.

Quite inexplicably Cassandra suddenly stopped quoting Hegel and seemed to go into a deeper trance.

"Well, that's a relief!" exclaimed Schiller. "I thought I might have to go over there and strangle her to get her to stop!"

As they waited to see what Cassandra might do next Herr Kolbe suddenly started acting strangely. It started with soft chuckles, as if he had thought of something funny—a private joke in his mind. This then progressed until he was soon laughing loudly, but for no apparent reason. Dodgson decided to move away from him and quietly made his way to an empty spot near the library door so that it would be easy to leave if things got out of hand.

Herr Kolbe abruptly stopped laughing, placed two fingers in his mouth and blew hard, creating an ear-splitting whistle. Everyone in the room immediately stopped their side-conversations and looked at him, not knowing what it was that he was whistling for or about.

"Cab!" he yelled, jumping up and down and waving his arms wildly as if trying to get the attention of something on the opposite side of the room. Everyone looked to where he was gesturing, wondering what he might be seeing. "Cab!" he screamed again. *"Kommen Sie hierher!"*

Inspector Spectre, who was still standing near Herr Kolbe, reached over and grabbed him firmly by the shoulders. "Herr Kolbe! Herr Kolbe! There's nothing there, Old Chap!"

"Was?" he asked, turning to Inspector Spectre to see why he had taken hold of his shoulders and was shaking him.

"There is no cab, Herr Kolbe! You're hallucinating!"

Herr Kolbe looked back to where he had just seen the cab. *"Ja!* Is cab! A coach *und vier Pferd."* He held up three lingers in Inspector Spectre's face. *"Vier schwarze Pferde!"* He looked back where he had just seen them. *"Was?* No, wait! Where have dey gone?" He stood up on tiptoe, as if trying to see better, then turning full circles like a ballerina, looking frantically in all directions. Suddenly he screamed and jumped behind Inspector Spectre, terrified at some new apparition. *"Schau! Mein Gott!"*

Inspector Spectre looked at the place where Herr Kolbe's stare was riveted, but could see nothing except mouldy books. He could feel Herr Kolbe's body trembling as he tied to hide behind him. "What do you see, Old Boy?" he demanded. "What is it?"

"*Der große Bär! Mit* no head!"

"A bear without a head?" Inspector Spectre asked. "You see a headless bear?"

"*Ja! Ja! Ohne Kopf!*" He screamed again.

"Speak English, Man! Speak English! You're not making any sense!"

"The bear," Herr Kolbe said, his eyes wide in terror, "hit has not the head! Only body! Look, you can see! Look!"

"No, I don't see!" said Inspector Spectre. "You're hallucinating!"

"The bear is hungry! He's very hungry! He's going to eat me!" He screamed again, pitifully.

"How is it going to eat you if it has no head?" demanded Inspector Spectre. "What's it going to bite you with? Snap out of it, Man! Snap out of it!"

"It's the gases, Sir Charles," Schiller said calmly to Inspector Spectre. "He's obviously been breathing too much elayl. We seem to have competing oracles."

Inspector Spectre looked back over at Cassandra who was still completely out. "You're probably right. There's probably been too much gas accumulating in the room. I'm going to go over and put the cork back in the pipe before we all get blown to kingdom come!"

"They're not going to like that!" Schiller cautioned. "You'll probably have a fight on your hands if you try it."

Inspector Spectre ignored him and rushed over to the Tripodial Throne of Prophesy and quickly corked the Oracular Tube. This caused a general uproar of protest from the crowd. "Take the cork out!" one rather burly man demanded, standing up in an aggressive manner. "What do you think you're doing? Take it out!"

"There's too much gas building up in the room!" Inspector Spectre tried to explain. "It's not safe!"

"Just who do you think you are?" the agitated man demanded. "You're not even a member! Take the cork out right now or I'm coming over there and making you eat it! We're not through listening to the Oracle."

"Yeah!" numerous other members assented.

"Uncork the tube!"

"Pull the plug!"

"I wo'n't!" Inspector Spectre said with resolve. "It's not safe!"

"That's it!" said the burly man, who made a rush for the Inspector, intent on punching him in the nose. He swung at the Inspector, and missed, the Inspector's police training making him quite capable of defending himself. When he turned to swing again the Inspector floored him with a hard right to the jaw.

The crowd went silent for a moment, stunned at what had just happened, but then, as if on signal, they rushed the Inspector *en masse* and quickly overpowered him. Six strong men grappled with the Inspector briefly, then taking hold of his arms and legs, carried him to the front door and bodily threw him out onto the pavement, slamming the door behind them.

The Inspector got to his feet, holding his painfully skinned knees and unsure what to do, convinced that the house might explode momentarily. He rushed back up to the door and was just ready to strike the knocker when the door opened and out stepped Dodgson with the lovely Cassandra slung over his shoulder like a sack of corn.

"I say!" exclaimed Inspector Spectre.

"I wouldn't go back in there, if I was you, Sir Charles. It's a bit of a riot!"

"What's happening?"

"Half of the members are hallucinating—seeing everything from kangaroos grinding coffee mills to elephants dancing while playing fifes. The other half is convulsed in hysterical laughter. I decided to bring Miss Pythia out for some fresh air before she expired from lack of oxygen."

"Good show! But we need to evacuate the house—open the windows. If the gases keep building there's a good chance the building will blow up like a Welsh coal mine!"

"There's far too many of them for us to force them out. You know what happened to you when you tried to cork the tube. We might try calling the police."

"I *am* the police!"

"What?"

"My real name is Inspector Ian Spectre of SOB."

"Inspector Inspector of SOB? What are you talking about?"

"SOB is a special branch of Scotland Yard. I'm here undercover to investigate the Oxford Phantasmalogical Society. The Yard has received numerous complaints. I can see why!"

"Are you telling me that you're not really Sir Charles Skeffingstone of Stranglebleat House?"

"That's right. I'm in disguise."

"Quite a good one!" Dodgson said. "You certainly had me fooled!"

"Thank you! Now, we really must do something. And quickly!"

"I am doing something!"

"What?"

"I'm rescuing Miss Pythia."

"Oh! Yes, I see that. Quite admirable, really. Why don't you just prop her up over there, against that wall away from the house—in case No. 42 blows up—and we'll go back in there and see if we can seal off the gases."

"That doesn't sound like something I really want to undertake."

"Come on, Man! We're those people's only hope! They're so intoxicated by the mysterious gases that they ca'n't help themselves! They're quite mad."

"I quite agree with you on that last point!"

"We ca'n't fight them, so we'll have to try to make our way into the cellar where the gases come from and open the damper on the chimney—see if we can get it pulling out the vapours again. Someone must have closed the damper."

"Sounds pretty risky to me. And it will be as dark as pitch in the cellar. We don't dare take a candle or a lamp with us."

"How hard can it be? It's just a cellar. We both know what a hearth feels like, and surely we can find the handle for the damper by touch!"

"Perhaps," Dodgson said, but sounded quite sceptical.

"We must try!"

"All right. Lead the way."

"Good! Quick, put Miss Pythia over there and let's go!"

Dodgson did as instructed and they both went back inside, the front door still ajar from when Dodgson had exited.

"Where's the cellar door?" Dodgson asked.

"I have no idea. I suppose it would be off the kitchen. Let's head down that way." As they passed the library they glanced inside. Almost everyone in the room was prophesying some nonsense or other.

They finally located the kitchen and the cellar door, which led down a narrow set of stairs.

"Watch yourself!" Inspector Spectre admonished. "Don't bump your head or fall down the stairs!"

The stairs were very narrow and very steep, and they made slow progress as they carefully felt their way down into the cellar in the inky blackness. The fumes of methane and ethene were quite thick and both men started having trouble breathing.

"We need to find the chimney quickly or we may be asphyxiated!" the Inspector said. "I'll go left and you go right. We'll meet in the middle. If you find the fireplace get the damper open as soon as you can!"

Dodgson pulled his shirt up over his face in a vain attempt to make it easier to breathe. "All right," he said in a muffled voice.

A minute later Inspector Spectre located the hearth. "Here it is! Over here! Come here quickly and help me find the damper!"

Dodgson headed for the Inspector's voice, and being a tall man, immediately bumped his head hard on a beam, cutting his scalp. "Ow!" he yelped, grabbing the top of his head. A small trickle of blood ran down his forehead and to the end of his nose, where it dripped onto his shirt. But he was soon on his way again, this time stooping over in an attempt to avoid banging his head again. They both felt around the mouldy walls until Dodgson finally located the handle and shoved it to what he hoped was the open position. "Got it!" he announced. The Inspector reached his arm up the chimney trying to feel if the damper was truly open.

"You did it!" he announced. "It's open. Let's get up to some air. I'm getting dizzy!"

It took them about a minute to retrace their way to the stairs and make their way up. They stumbled into the kitchen and then both ran for the front door and fresh air. Once outside they made their way over to where Miss Pythia was still propped and collapsed against the wall. The Inspector and Dodgson were both gasping for air like just-landed fish.

"That was horrible!" Dodgson said when he finally had his breath back. "I never want to go into another cellar as long as I live!"

The Inspector nodded. "You're right! Terrible! I thought we were goners there at the end. I wasn't sure I could even make it to the top of the stairs!"

"What about all of those people still inside?" Dodgson asked.

"I don't know," he admitted. "We need to get them out—they're still in grave danger—but how?"

Dodgson thought for a moment. "I have an idea!"

"What is it?"

"I'll go back inside and begin giving my lecture on Symbolic Logic. I suspect that most people will immediately get up and leave rather than listen to it."

"Brilliant idea!" agreed the Inspector. "Try the Barbershop Problem on them."

Dodgson got back to his feet and went back inside, first making his way over to the Tripod and corking the pipe. The audience was still in hysterics—some prophesying the end of the world—others, that man would one day walk on the moon. Many members were simply euphoric—giggling and laughing uncontrollably. A few were sitting trance-like, staring into deep inner-space at fascinating displays of colour.

Without further ado Dodgson launched loudly into his introductory lecture on Symbolic Logic, Part II, which he knew by heart. Twenty minutes later the only people remaining were Mr Schiller and Mrs Wilcox, who was carrying on an intimate conversation with a demon spirit that she mistakenly believed to be her dear departed Nick.

Dodgson went over to Schiller. "If you'll give me a hand we might be able to get Mrs Wilcox out the front door."

"OK, I'll do what I can. By the way, I was quite enjoying your lecture."

"Thank you."

"Do you realize that you've been injured? You have a streak of dried blood running down your forehead and all the way down to the tip of your nose."

Dodgson wiped at his forehead and nose. "I bumped my head on a beam in the cellar."

"What on earth were you doing in the cellar?"

"Sir Charles and I concluded that everyone in the house was in danger. The concentration of gases had built up dangerously high. So, we made our way down into the cellar and opened the damper on a fireplace down there to ventilate the cellar and reduce the inflow of gases into the library, but we couldn't figure out how to evacuate the building. I decided that if I started lecturing on symbolic logic that everyone would eventually get so bored they would leave."

Schiller started laughing, finding this all quite hilarious.

"It worked!" Dodgson said. "Except for you and Mrs Wilcox, of course. We really do need to get her out of here. The gases may still be at a dangerous concentration!"

"All right, let's give it a go!"

They both tried their level best to convince Mrs Wilcox with logic and philosophical reasoning to leave. Finally, they even tried to pick her up bodily and lead her to the door, but she lay down on the floor and went limp, and there was simply no way that the two of them could move her eighteen-stone bulk any more than they could drag a stranded whale off of a beach at low tide.

"Madame!" Dodgson said, making one last effort. "The house is in danger of exploding. We really must leave now!"

Mrs Wilcox would not relent. "I'm talking to Nick. I'll leave when we're through—not a moment sooner!"

"Mrs Wilcox, if we don't leave immediately you may well land in his very lap when you are blown into eternity!"

"I refuse!" she said with finality. "I shall not be moved!"

"Very well, Madame, we leave you to your fate! Come on, Mr Schiller, I suggest that we immediately remove ourselves from the premises!"

Schiller nodded and they both ran for the front door. When they emerged they found that the moon was up and they could see that the street now looked like the main corridor in a lunatic asylum. OPS members were walking up and down the street making insane prophecies about moving photographs and transistors, while others laughed hysterically at what they were saying. Inspector Spectre was valiantly trying to herd them as far away from No. 42 as possible, but they kept wandering back like daft sheep.

Dodgson and Schiller had hardly left the house when there was a deafening explosion as the ethene-filled house exploded. Enormous fireballs blew out through every window, from cellar to the third floor attic. Glass and shattered shutters flew through the air, striking the buildings on the opposite side of the street. The front door was blown off of its hinges.

Luckily no one happened to be directly in front of the house when it blew up. Frightened OPS members had dived for the pavement or behind anything they could find for cover. Fortunately, the building's old stone walls were thick enough to absorb the blast and didn't crumble into the street, much of the force effectively vented through the shattered windows and door.

Mrs Wilcox's shade, launched into eternity by the force of the blast, landed in Purgatory on a particularly hot bed of coals, right next to the shade of Georg Wilhelm Friedrich Hegel and just a briquette's throw away from the shade of Karl Marx, not so much to punish her for necromancy, but rather to punish the two philosophers for the woes wrought on the earth through their insidious dialectics.

Rushing over to see if the lovely Miss Cassandra Pythia had in any way been injured by the flying glass, Dodgson was surprised to find her sitting on the curbstone, once more delivering prophecies, her system evidently still containing adequate residuals of elayl. When she noticed him she said,

"In your old age you will write a novel about fairies, filled with insipid conversation and nauseating romance that will be universally panned."

But since the prophetess was named Cassandra, Dodgson naturally didn't believe her.

Obituary: *The Cincinnati Midwesterner* (p. D–4), 9 August 1937

DR. F. C. S. SCHILLER, PHILOSOPHER, PASSES SILENTLY INTO THE ABSOLUTE

***

USC and Corpus Christi, Oxford Professor "Deader than Hegel"

***

Famous author of "Riddles of the Sphinx: and "Mind!" Parody

***

LOS ANGELES, Aug. 8 (UPS).—Dr. Ferdinand Canning Scott Schiller died at home yesterday after a short illness. He was 73. Funeral services were held today. Surviving is his widow, Mrs Louise Schiller, a "child-friend" whom he had married only two years ago.

—

Dr. Schiller was born on Aug. 16, 1864 in Schleswig-Holstein. He was educated at Rugby School and Balliol College, Oxford, where he received the MA degree. At various times in his life he taught logic and metaphysics at Corpus Christi College, Oxford, Cornell University (1893-1897), and the University of Southern California (1929»37). He was Pres. of the Aristotelian Society and the British Society for Psychical Research, a Fellow of the British Academy, and a member of the mysterious Oxford Phantasmalogical Society (OPS).

Schiller was known to have suffered much of his adult life from lung disease, said to have been initiated by hyper-exposure to ethene gas at an OPS meeting in 1881 in which a member, posing as a modern Delphenic Oracle, attempted to prophesy under the influence of this gas which was emitted from the cellar. He narrowly escaped with his life when the highly flammable gas exploded.

Schiller was the primary British exponent of pragmatism, having co-founded the Pragmatic School of Philosophy with William James and John Dewey. Schiller spent a great deal of his life debunking and ridiculing the philosophy of Georg Wilhelm Friedrich Hegel (1770–1831) through his extensive writing and polemical debates with the so-called "Absolute Idealists" such as F. H. Bradley and Bertrand Russell. He considered himself a "Humanist", declaring that

"Truth is whatever proves to be valuable to the individual."

Schiller wrote an enormous number of books, pamphlets and articles, including his anonymous "Riddles of the Sphinx" (1891), expressing anti-materialism and nonskeptical relativism, "Axioms as Postulates" (1902), in which he announced his version of pragmatism, and "Humanism" (1903). He also authored the influential "Cassandra, or the Future of the British Empire" (1926), whose title reportedly owes as much to Homer as it does to a strange event involving a latter day Cassandra figure in the mysterious OPS. Schiller eloquently expressed the age-old question "Must Philosophers Disagree?" (1934). The answer, as everyone already knew, was "Yes." The "Hegel Colouring Book: Colour Me Grey," long ascribed to Schiller, is now thought to be a forgery.

Most of his writings are extremely boring and little known outside academia, but his marvelous, influential parody issue of "Mind", cleverly entitled "Mind!" (1901), has been widely read and acclaimed. This included the hysterical article "A Commentary on the *Snark*", which he pseudonymously authored as Snarkophilus Snobbs, humorously purporting to explain Lewis Carroll's classic nonsense epic poem, *The Hunting of the Snark* (1876), and equating the Boojum Snark and Hegel's "Absolute".

> "In the midst of the ward he was trying
>   to say,
> In the midst of his laughter and glee,
> He had softly and silently vanished
>   away—
> For the Snark was a Boojum you see."
>   —Lewis Carroll

ALSO AVAILABLE FROM EVERTYPE

Eachtraí Eilíse i dTír na nIontas, *Alice* in Irish, 2007

Lastall den Scáthán agus a bhFuair Eilís Ann Roimpi
Looking-Glass in Irish, 2009

Le Avventure di Alice nel Paese delle Meraviglie
Alice in Italian, 2010

L's Aventuthes d'Alice en Êmèrvil'lie
Alice in Jersey French, 2012

Alicia in Terra Mirabili, *Alice* in Latin, 2011

Alice ehr Eventüürn in't Wunnerland
Alice in Low German, 2010

Contoyrtyssyn Ealish ayns Çheer ny Yindyssyn
Alice in Manx, 2010

Dee Erläwnisse von Alice em Wundalaund
Alice in Mennonite German, 2012

L'Aventuros de Alis in Marvoland, *Alice* in Neo, 2012

Ailice's Àventurs in Wunnerland, *Alice* in Scots, 2011

Alices Äventyr i Sagolandet, *Alice* in Swedish, 2010

Alice's Carrànts in Wunnerlan, *Alice* in Ulster Scots, 2011

Ventürs jiela Lälid in Stunalän, *Alice* in Volapük, 2012

Anturiaethau Alys yng Ngwlad Hud, *Alice* in Welsh, 2010